Snow-Kissed

LAURA FLORAND

Chapter 1

The snow fell over the black granite counter in a soft hush of white. Kai focused on the sieve she shook as she brought a winter of sugar to the dark world, letting the powder slide across her thoughts the way snow on a falling night would, taking all with it, even her, leaving only peace.

That peace lay so cold. She had almost forgotten how cold she felt, until he showed up.

The man who, once upon a time, had always made her so warm and happy.

Now he stood at the window, looking as cold as she was. Destroying all peace. Past him and the pane of glass, only a few flakes fell against a gray sky, rare and disinterested, nature as usual failing her. Her fall of powdered sugar could not come between her and him, could not blur him to some distant place cut off by the arrival of winter. Could not hush him, if ever he chose to speak.

No, all she could do was concentrate on the sugar-snow. Looking up—looking at him—undid everything.

"I don't think they're coming," the man said finally, and she swallowed. It was funny how her whole body ached at his voice. As if her skin had gotten unused to his vibrations running over it. As if she needed to develop tiny calluses at the base of every hair follicle so that those hairs would not want to shiver.

Light brown hair neatly cut, he stood angled toward the window, shoulders straight, with that long, intellectual fitness he had, the over-intelligent, careful man who had played sports almost like he might study for a test, maintaining perfect physical fitness as just another one of his obligations. She still remembered when he had discovered Ultimate Frisbee, the awkward, unfamiliar, joy-filled freedom in him as he explored the idea of playing something so intense *just for fun*. It had been rather beautiful. She had gone to all his games and chatted with the other wives with their damn babies and even played on his pick-up teams sometimes, although unwilling to put forth the effort to be part of his competitive leagues.

Those fun, fun years full of weekends of green grass, and friendly people, and laughter. They had had too many happy days. They clogged in her all the sudden, dammed up too tight, hurting her.

She had screwed them all the fuck up. Forever.

She didn't know what to say to him, after what she had done, so she concentrated on shedding snow, like some great, dangerous goddess bending over her granite world, a creature half-formed from winter clouds, drifting eerily apart from all humanity. She wished he had not come, but the thought of him leaving wrenched a hole in her that filled up instantly with tears.

Hot, liquid tears that sloshed around inside her and wanted to spill out. That in itself was terrifying and strange; she had thought she had tamed her tears down to something near-solid and quiescent, a slushy of grief that lay cold in her middle but no longer spilled out at every wrong movement, every careless glimpse of happy couples or children laughing in a park.

She had so hoped that she had reached a point where she could—see him. Where all that long process of coming to peace with herself and her losses would be strong enough to withstand a glimpse of him. But all of her, every iota of strength and peace, had dissolved into pain and longing the instant she saw him step out of his car, a flake of snow catching on his hair.

Damn it, his mother was supposed to be here. She was supposed to come with her magazine staff for this shoot, a whole entourage to make it easier on both Kai and Kurt. How could they have abandoned her to this reopening of wounds because they were afraid of a few flakes of snow?

she focused with all her strength. She had to get this sugar exactly right, not too thick, not too shallow, not too even, not too ragged, leaving perfect graceful curves and fades into black at its edges. It was soothing to work on that white against gleaming black. To focus on those tiny grains, almost as tiny as cells of life.

She could control these grains. She could always get them right. If she worked hard enough. If she really, really tried.

"The snow is supposed to start from the south and close us off," Kurt said from the window. "They probably didn't want to chance it."

Now why would Anne Winters's staff do that to her? Leave her alone with him just to avoid bad roads? Those selfish people, it was almost as if they had . . . families. Reasons to live that were far more important than she was.

Kurt shifted enough to watch her, but she didn't look up. She shouldn't have let him come, but for God's sake, his mother was Anne Winters. First of all, Anne had only rented the cabin to Kai so affordably on the condition that Kai maintain it for her use in photo shoots when she wanted it. And even without that agreement, Kai was a food stylist who regularly contracted to Anne Winters's company. She could hardly refuse this photo shoot for next year's holiday edition, Anne's biggest. And accepting it, she had to jump through Anne's hoops, even the famous multi-tasker's insistence on having her lawyer son with her for the weekend so she could work on contract negotiations simultaneously. Her formidable presence and the bustle of her staff should have helped dissipate all this miasma from their past and saved them from any need to linger in it.

Besides, Kai was supposed to be strong enough for this now. She had worked so hard to heal, to grow strong. To still and chill those tears down to something—bearable.

"Are you ready to be snowed in?" Kurt asked. "Do you want me to run to the store and pick up any supplies while there's still a chance?"

Her stomach tightened as if he had just pierced it with some long, strange, beautiful shard of ice. *Kurt. Don't take care of me. You always did that so, so*—the ice shard slid slowly through her inner organs, slicing, hurting—*well.*

"Why don't you check your email so that you'll know for sure whether they've cancelled?" he suggested. "Or find your charger so I can check my phone?" They had matching smartphones; their shared two-year contract still hadn't expired.

She didn't check her email or find her charger mostly because she didn't dare leave this powdered sugar snow. She had to keep her focus. She had to.

She hadn't yet managed to say a word to him. When she had opened the door, she had meant to. It shouldn't have been so hard. *Hello, Kurt.* She could say that, right? After practicing it over and over in her head on the way to the door. But the instant their eyes met, his hazel gaze had struck her mute. As the moment drew out, his hand had clenched around his duffle until his knuckles showed white, and his whole body leaned just an inch forward, as it had so many, many times in their lives, when she greeted him after a long day or a trip, and he leaned in to kiss her.

She had flinched back so hard that her elbows had rapped the foyer wall with a resounding smack, and he had looked away from her and walked quickly into the cabin without speaking, disappearing to find a room for his things. It had been at least twenty minutes before he reappeared, his hands in his pockets, to set himself at that post by the window and watch the road. Probably sending out a desperate mental call to his mother: *Hurry up, God damn it. Where the hell are you?*

But the cars hadn't come, and now he watched her. She could feel his gaze trying to penetrate her concentration on the snow. But she had to get that powdered sugar snow just right. She had to. Even if she had to play at snow for all eternity.

"Kai," he said and she shivered. Her name. Her name in his voice. "Can you still not even look at me?"

The weariness in his voice was like a hook dragging her gaze to him, and she did get her head up, just for a second, because he deserved so much better from her than what she had managed to give him. But he was so beautiful and so distant there against the window that it broke her heart, and her heart was so tired of being broken. It gave up quickly and let her look down at her sugar-snow again.

"Do you want me to go?" he asked.

Oh, God, yes. Oh, God, no. Oh, God, she didn't know. *It's snowing,* she wanted to protest, but her lips felt stiff and frozen. Besides, it was snowing more on her counter than it was outside. He could get away still, if he wanted.

"Kai." He sounded as exhausted as her heart. But— firm against that exhaustion. Determined to go on through it. He was that way.

She concentrated as hard as she could.

"It was the cruelest thing you ever did to me," he told her evenly. "When you cut me off like this. And you never even told me why."

Her heart seized. Her eyes stung, as if it was a year and a half ago again. She set the sieve to the side and considered the effect of the sugar.

"Can you tell me why now?" He had developed that even voice in law school or maybe in boardrooms afterward or maybe just growing up in his mother's household. No matter what the tensions or what was at stake, he could manage to stay steady, calm. No one who knew him would ever believe the fights they had had, there at the end of all things. Once she had even made him weep. "Or is it still too soon?"

She grabbed the edge of a wax paper snowflake

stencil too clumsily and left her fingerprint in the snow around it. Damn it, she hated it when she messed things up. Once she had been able to tolerate her mistakes, be patient with herself as she fixed them, but then everything had gone to hell and she had to—she *had to*—at least get something like the damn sugar snow right.

It was only in the past few months that she had started to calm that raging intolerance toward herself back into something sane again. She had worked so hard for that calm. She had taken so many long walks and deep breaths and forced her mind to think so many beautiful, strong thoughts. Now Kurt at the window had made all her intolerance surge up again, intensely, like its last stand.

"I just couldn't," she said low, to her finger smudge in the snow. Her voice sounded rough, unused. She talked to people up here—her support group, her clients—but it had been a year and a half since she talked to him. Or fought. Funny, a year and a half later, the first sounds out of her mouth sounded as if her voice was still rubbed raw from screaming. "I couldn't open up anymore, I couldn't try. I just couldn't." *I'm sorry, I'm sorry, I'm so sorry.* She fought not to bow her body over the granite, not to clutch the edge and ruin all her work, in a plea for forgiveness for something else she had ruined beyond recall.

She had begged for pardon everywhere, after the second miscarriage. *I'm sorry, I'm so sorry, what's wrong with me, what did I do wrong, doctors, tell me what to do.*

Kurt had told her it didn't matter. He had said that, stroking her hair back from her wet cheeks as if he was trying to do a good thing: *"Kai, it doesn't matter. Don't worry about it."* Yes, he had said that. It had been true for him.

The third miscarriage had been the end. The end of her hope. The end of her. The end of them.

She didn't even want forgiveness. Forgiveness hurt.

A moment's silence. His hands in his pockets, his body long and straight, he watched her, even more intensely contained than she remembered. "I didn't ask you to try. In fact, I told you to stop trying."

That old pain swelled up in her so hard she couldn't understand why it didn't just break her. She had begged it, so many times, to break her, to go ahead and split her apart so she didn't have to be anymore. "I know."

She drew a breath. Grief and its pain came in waves; after a time she had learned the grief counselors were right about that. This was just one of those waves, kicked up high by him, her world's earthquake over there by the window. The calm was on the other side of it and would come back in a moment. Maybe after he left. Oh, God. And the snow would fall, and there she would be, watching it as it cut her off from all the world, her arms wrapped around her knees.

Three months after she left him—maybe when he finally accepted she wasn't coming back—he had sold their house, without talking to her about it. It had been in his name, bought just before they met. Half the proceeds had appeared in her bank account, and information on a storage account and the code to access it had arrived in a formal printed letter, as if an email might bring them too close, might encourage a response. She had never gone to look at the storage, because . . . what if, in his over-careful way, he had decided he didn't have the right to get rid of the baby things for her? Or what if he had packed up their wedding photos? The terror of that had stuffed itself down her throat and choked her.

For weeks on end after that, she avoided her mailbox, but every time she steeled herself to work through its pile of envelopes, no notice of divorce proceedings had ever arrived. She still braced for it, every time. And it still never came. Maybe for him, too, divorce was a last wrenching, heart-breaking act he couldn't quite stand to face. When he did finally move to divorce her, it would doubtless mean he had met someone else, a new, fresh love who motivated him to clean up his past so that he could move on from it for the new woman's sake. At a distance, Kai had gotten used to that idea. She even knew that she should actually want that for him, a new, bright love without all the stains she had left on theirs. She was supposed to want that for him. It was her fault she had made him so unhappy.

Some of the money from the sale of the house had gone to rent this luxury cabin from his mother, and she had sat up here, with her arms wrapped around her knees, watching the snow fall, so peaceful, so freeing, shutting her off from everything, including him. She had thought the grief would kill her then. That she would literally die and no one find her body until spring. But it hadn't worked out that easy.

"But I couldn't stop," she said, and her breath came out too hard, skittering sugar across the granite landscape.

He nodded and looked out the window, hands in his pockets. He had such a beautiful body. It had always worked just right for her, that long, rangy over-analyzed athleticism, the way he could keep it so carefully fit and yet not quite know how to have fun with it, until he met her. She remembered, still, the first time he had ever burst into laughter for her. It had been their third date, two weeks after they met at his mother's enormous estate while Kai was setting up a spring flower-food photo shoot for Anne in her beautiful gardens.

For their third date, Kai had suggested a hike, because Kurt's carefully planned dinners just weren't working out the way their instinctive rapport in those gardens had suggested they would. Fascinated though she was by his over-thinking, she had wanted to get him away from it for a little while. They had rested in a glade on that gently sunny afternoon, him stretched out with his arms behind his head, thoughtful and serious, and her sitting with her legs folded, knees nearly but not quite brushing his ribs, fingers just itching to touch that stretched-out body, the body that he so carefully did not offer to her because he was so busy plotting how to get his approach to her just right that he didn't realize how right for her it already was.

And finally she had just reached out and dove her fingers with devilish precision into his ribs. He had twisted uncontrollably—she had *known* someone that careful had to be ticklish—and then burst out laughing. He had grabbed her wrists to stop her and when that pulled her body into a lean over his, looked up into her face with his hazel eyes brilliant with that unexpected laughter and something else, something even more hungry and delighted. It had been the first time they kissed. (Because he was *so careful*, so courteously respectful when he said good night those first two dinners.) If a couple of hikers hadn't passed about fifteen minutes later, it would have been the first time they made love, too.

He'd always liked to make love outside in the grass when he could find a spot, ever after. It just always seemed to make him so happy.

She'd always seemed to make him happy. As if she brought ease and laughter into his whole life.

Until she hadn't.

Until she had destroyed all that ease and taken all his laughter with it.

It had been the most terrible thing in her life that she had ever done. Her body had killed three other dreams of laughter and life and happiness, but at least she hadn't had control over those acts.

She wiped the smudge mark she had made completely clean with a bit of sponge, then took a tiny pinch of powdered sugar and rubbed it between her fingers to let it fall over that cleaned spot, hoping to repair the damage in a way that did not show, that would not make her start the whole thing over. Did that look right? Sometimes she focused on a food styling issue so long that she lost all perspective.

She removed the other four snowflake wax patterns without smudges and stood back to evaluate the look of the black granite forms showing through the white sugar. Were the snowflakes a too obvious choice? Should it be Christmas trees? That seemed so facile. Stars maybe? If she did some stars eight-pointed and some six-pointed, to reach more than one demographic, would that make the holiday shot over-reaching, ruining the whole effect?

"It was always fascinating to me," Kurt said, that steady, modulated voice of his just *hurting* her skin, "how you were so cheerful and careless everywhere else, as if life was pure fun and you weren't going to let anxiety over details get in the way of embracing every glorious part of it. And yet when you set up a shoot, you were always so obsessively careful. As if you, too, under all that fun, felt the same need to get everything, somewhere, exactly right."

He had such perfect diction, so New England, so educated. But he was never cruel with it, not on purpose, not like the infamous devastation his mother could wreak with a few cutting words, when people did not perform to her standards.

That had always been one of the things Kai loved about him so much: the way she could see his mother in him in a thousand small and big ways, and yet there was this kindness that was the very opposite of what his mother was known for, as if he had made a deliberate choice, in the face of great environmental odds, to be someone whose goodness was personal and direct and one-on-one, whose interactions were honorable and reliable and did no damage. All his choices had always been thought-out and conscious and deliberate, except that one choice—which wasn't really a choice, was it? rather a thing that swept over a person's life and changed it—to fall in love with her.

Her throat closed, and she couldn't talk anymore. Not to him. Not ever again to him. She didn't deserve him.

"You've lost so much weight," Kurt said. "Haven't you learned to love food again yet?"

No. She still could love its looks, the way she could get it absolutely right for a photograph, but that urge that had always kept those extra twenty pounds rounding her hips—to taste everything around her in those photo shoots, to tilt her head back and just sink into all those delicious flavors—had died. She had lost the people she cooked for casually—him, her friends, her family, all of whom she had fled—and so she had stopped cooking altogether. She hadn't realized until she was getting by on peanut butter and jelly sandwiches, alone, chewing mechanically, that enjoyment of food really depended on a belief in life and a belief that you could nourish it.

And who could believe in that?

All three of the pregnancies had left her so viciously nauseated, as if her body was some war zone, and she had always thought, if only she could have made peace with the food, if only she could have kept some of it down, things might have turned out differently, that getting her body to accept the food and getting her body to accept the pregnancy were the same thing. The doctors had said it didn't work that way, that it wasn't a mind-game she could control, but . . . the sense of failure and enmity remained. Food had let her down. Had betrayed her, when she least expected it. Had not nourished life.

"I wonder if I did the right thing, waiting," Kurt said low, his hands curled in his pockets.

Her heart tightened. She took a breath and managed to speak, to release him from this hell: "If you're worried about the snow, go ahead and go. You're probably right, that they're not coming." She couldn't blame him for wanting to get away before he got stuck for days alone with her. She had hurt him so much. The utter devastation of all that happiness he had found in her.

When Anne had succeeded in convincing him to come so that she could work on contracts and this winter wonderland magazine shoot at the same time, Kai had thought his agreement meant that he, too, had moved on. That he had managed to reduce his tears, too, to this half-frozen quiet inside him. That he was at a place where he could see her again and survive it. Maybe he had met that woman who would make him happy again and he wanted to broach the discussion on divorce.

She had tried hard to get ready for it, to be brave enough for it. She had reminded herself that she, too, had moved on, not to someone else—God, no, *never* again to open herself up that way—but to a calm, healed place. Or it had felt calm, it had felt healed, that cold slushy of grief had been almost comfortable, until he got there before everyone else did and she stood at the window watching him get out of his car, his long body moving with such controlled grace.

She set her equipment on the counter behind her, studying the snowfall of powdered sugar and its snowflakes. If Anne and her team weren't coming, none of this really mattered, but she couldn't let it go. She had to get it right. It was the only thing she had left to hold on to.

Silence stretched between them, the inside of the cabin as soft and as still as snow falling on an ancient forest. That silence was soothing. It was better. *No, let's not talk. Let's make at least that one thing easier on both of us. You can just go, Kurt. It's—it's okay.*

I'll manage to survive it somehow. I've survived everything else.

Yes, one thing she had learned about herself that she had never known before: that she did, in fact, survive things she hadn't thought she could possibly bear.

Kurt left the window, and she startled. Scarier still, he didn't head out of the room but straight toward her. By the time he reached the other side of the island, her heart was beating so hard she thought she might be sick with it. *Don't try to kiss me good-bye or anything, Kurt. Not even on the cheek. Please don't.*

Don't say anything, like, "Well, I hope you have a happy life." Or, "Good-bye, Kai." Please, please don't.

She didn't look at him, willing the message onto him, willing him away. But she could feel him looking at her.

He took one hand out of his pocket and slowly drew his finger across some of the sugar, and indignation surprised its way through her fear. It was not at all like Kurt to destroy someone's work that way.

He circled the island, with the sugar still on his finger. She froze, so terribly afraid at his approach that she could have been cowering before the advent of some horrible torturer.

He stopped just behind her, and she bowed her head, all the hairs of her body on end.

Without a word, he ran his palm down the length of her arm—a full, firm stroke that shocked all through her—until he came to her exposed wrist, the sleeves pulled back for her work. There he drew the sugar gently across the exquisitely sensitive inside of her wrist, a magical brush of callused fingertip and powder. Kai gasped, her whole body poised in astonishment, as if she was balancing on a cliff's edge via one toe on the head of a pin.

Kurt brought her wrist to his mouth and sucked the sugar off.

She gasped again, collapsing, her other hand smashing into that sugar snowfall to hold her up. *Kurt, what are you doing? Kurt—wait, what?*

He licked her wrist clean of sugar, little sucking sips with his tongue that were so delicate it was as if this tall, controlled, strong man behind her was a butterfly and she was nectar.

Her eyes went blind. What was this? What was this—sudden, incredible warmth and sensuality crossing an impossible distance? The bridge across that distance was burned, wasn't it burned?

Still with no sound, Kurt drew the index finger of his other hand through more sugar, leaving a path under one of her snowflakes, and—

Stroked a little figure eight of it over her nape. She shivered, the touch washing from her nape through her whole body. And he bent and sucked that off, too.

Kai folded into the counter, shaking all over, the warmth so great and sudden that it *hurt*, it hurt so horribly, like life coming back to a frozen limb. This couldn't be happening. Why in the world would he *do* this?

His mouth traveled up her neck and down, once, twice, and then all at once it pressed into her suddenly hard, until she could feel the edge of his teeth and the tension in his body, as if he was about to *bite* her, in some animal show of dominance. Which was not like Kurt *at all*, and yet that edge in him ran all through her, loosening muscles, loosening thought.

He gentled again, the tension still in his body but not in his mouth, so that her own body didn't know which would win, his tension or his gentleness. Such a tantalizing knife's edge. She wanted to fall on both sides.

Oh, but that would cut her right in two. She would never get the pieces of herself back together again.

He licked the nape of her neck, that tiny, teasing lick and suck, taking her wrist and bringing her sugar-smeared hand over her shoulder. The move wrapped her arm around herself, his own folded over it, her vulnerable insides so thoroughly protected by both of them. And while she was held in that double warmth, he swirled his tongue in the center of her palm, licked his way up her index finger, and then drew it deep into his mouth.

She stared half-blind across her snowscape at the great window giving onto the deep gray sky, a winter queen yanked down out of her swirling cold clouds into a human embrace. She had forgotten what it felt like, to be warm, to be alive, to be touched. My God, had all this once been *familiar?*

He took his time on that finger, lavishing it with his attention, long, strong suckles until her weight caved into the arm that held her—all hard muscle. If anything, he had gotten fitter and more intense since the last time his body had been pressed against hers. More driven.

He sucked his way from finger to finger, while all her body melted in some panicked rush of failing winter, *I'm not ready for spring, no, I'm not ready!* He set her cleaned hand down on her own shoulder—curling it there with a protective stroke, as if he knew she needed to hug herself. Then his hand swept through her snowscape again. Her heart tightened and tightened, and her body shivered in expectation as his sugar-dusted hand rose . . . to her throat, rubbing the sugar slowly into that so-sensitive skin.

Heat and fear and longing swept her at that promise of what was coming.

Wrapping one hand in her ponytail, he turned her, pulling her head back until her body bent over his arm. Her heart was beating so hard, emotion, anticipation, arousal, terror pounding through her everywhere as she stared up at him. His eyes met hers just briefly, just that shock of intimacy, her beautiful secret, those hazel eyes of his. And then he bent his head again and cleaned that sugar off her exposed throat.

She began to shake under the onslaught of sensuality and warmth, shake with the mad tremors of someone coming out of hypothermia, as he pulled her sweater over her head and undid her bra. For a moment after he threw both garments away, he stood there, staring down at her, his hands pressed to the island on either side of her, that look in his eyes so strange and yet familiar, not the Kurt she had known for years with the seriousness that turned into laughter for her, but the Kurt she had left at the end, with that desperate intensity in his eyes. *Kai, don't. Kai, don't do this.*

He lifted hands covered with powdered sugar to her breasts, leaving black granite handprints among the black snowflakes in her sugar-snow. That familiar, long-lost caress as he cupped her sent an ache all through her, as if her breasts had been too tightly bound for more than a year now and finally, finally been freed. She whimpered, and he rubbed powdered thumbs over her nipples, knowing what she wanted, knowing how she loved to have her breasts cupped and caressed, knowing how that made her sigh for him and pet him and want him.

Her hands came up and caught at his shoulders, leaving white prints on his shirt. Pressing her breasts higher, he bent—oh, how her whole body knew exactly what was coming and her nipples strained for it—and closed his mouth around her, devouring the sweetness like someone who was starved. Like someone who had not had anything sweet for a long, long time.

Her breath came in short, sharp pants, leaving her dizzy in the whirl of warmth and heat. She couldn't do this. She couldn't. That slushy of grief and loss inside her sloshed so dangerously. If everything that was frozen about her melted, there might not be anything left of her at all.

A snow-woman. A statue of ice. Come face to face with the sun.

Oh, God.

He leaned her backward on the counter, still licking and sucking over her breasts, under them, pushing up the fullness to make sure he had every last dusting of sugar, even as he lay her back into more sugar. He pulled down her jeans and panties both at once, pushing them to the floor. Now she was entirely naked except for sugar, and he was entirely clothed. The only marks she had left on him were the handprints on his shoulders.

He still had not said one word. She could not have spoken if her life depended on it, which she very much felt it did. *No, see, please. This is going to hurt like hell.*

I was—calm before. I had reached this place where I could be at peace. Where I even understood that I had lost all right to you.

He scraped up a handful of sugar from her counter and sprinkled it in a gentle tickling kiss of powder from her knee up her thigh. *Oh-oh-oh.* She tried to squeeze herself shut, her eyes, her sex, her fists, her toes, but he bent and put his mouth to her knee, and that was, *oh, God, so sweet.* He followed that trail of sugar all the way up her thigh, and everything in her dissolved, uncurled—toes, fists, sex. Even her eyelids grew soft and languorous, flickering open and falling closed again, in a blur of him and darkness.

He didn't use sugar on her sex.

He just spread her thighs on that dark smooth granite dusted with powder and tasted her exactly as she was.

Oh, God. Oh, God.

She was falling and scrambling, hands sliding over slick granite and fine powder and finding no purchase, tumbling into vertigo all while held so adamantly on stone. It was not that he had never done this, but— well, she didn't usually *like* it, she would rather they be kissing each other's *mouths*—and, and, and—her mind kept dissolving into all these golden hot swirls of not-thought, this being, this warm, warm sense of being—

So, so—

It was just too mu—

The very last thing she had expected of her life that day was to find herself coming, in a rush of gloriousness, dissolving for him, mindless, convulsing. He forced that glory through her and wouldn't let it *stop*, his mouth on her so driven, so intense that she had to whimper and pull her legs up onto the counter, curling inward, to get him to let her orgasm subside.

Only then did he allow her to come down from it, burying his face in her ribs.

She lay boneless and damp and hot on granite so hard and cold. He straightened slowly, as if every muscle in his body hurt. She couldn't look at him. Just this flicker of her eyelashes that showed him to her: completely dressed, her only mark on him two prints of powdered sugar on his shoulders and the voluptuousness of his mouth, as he stood over her sugar-dusted nakedness, stroking her slowly, breasts to belly, down her spine, over her hips, those gentle, reassuring touches he had long ago learned she needed, after sex, the ones that made her feel so loved, that told her that he still found her body beautiful after he was done wanting it. He had always done that for her, once he knew she needed it, always, always, always, made sure to take his time afterward, to stroke her and caress her before he fell asleep or left the bed.

Except he wasn't done wanting, was he? He hadn't come—had he? He was still completely dressed. Her gaze skated down his body, and—no, he hadn't come.

She could not think. She bent her arms to hide her face. But then she had to look at him again, because— well, she had to see.

Their eyes held. His were so gorgeous, their beauty all for her, her special treasure that no one else had the sense to see. You had to know him so well to know the color of his eyes; his friends couldn't even remember it, and yet she had always known, right from the first moment he stood looking down at her in his mother's gardens and she looked back up into those hazel eyes, and her heart caught.

Her heart had been so smart. Suicidal in its bright optimism, clueless as to what would come, but still—so smart, to so immediately respond to him.

He had deserved her heart. He had deserved better.

From the very first, he had always been so careful to give her the very best of himself.

She was the one. She was the one who hadn't been able to give him something good enough back. It had been her *job* to be happy, it was what she brought to their couple, it was who she *was* in life, the happy person, and then, and then . . .

She drew a breath in and sighed it out, shaky, shivery. She was so entirely naked here on this granite. All illusion of distance gone.

And yet she hadn't melted out of existence, as she expected. Life *never* let her escape just by destroying her completely, no matter how convinced she was, in the moment, that she was being destroyed.

"I probably shouldn't have done that," he said low, touching a streak of sugar on her cheek. His beautiful eyes were so very close, his expression driven, torn. "I don't know anymore. I don't think I've gotten anything right since you first got pregnant." His fingers sifted her hair, sticking now from the sugar. "It made me realize that you were always the one who got us right. Who made us happy." His mouth twisted on such a hard-contained wave of grief and pain that she wanted to catch him in a tight fist, say, *No! It wasn't* you. *It was* me. *I was the one who went wrong.* "I tried, though." He stepped away from her.

A moment later, still lying there naked on a counter in powdered sugar, she heard the front door open and close.

And Kai curled into a fetal ball, pulling sugar-coated arms over her face and bending sugar-coated legs into her naked belly, and wept until she couldn't weep anymore.

Chapter 2

Heavy, ragged, *hot* sobs like she had cried for the second miscarriage and never been able to cry since, not even for the third, not even when she left Kurt, when the tears had been weak, exhausted things that would come out of nowhere and slide aimlessly down her cheeks, as if they didn't even have the strength left in them to heal.

A long time passed before the discomfort of the granite got to her, and the cold of her naked body, and the stickiness of sugar melted by sweat and tears into her skin and hair. Finally she peeled herself off the island to take a shower. The water had been running over her for a good five minutes before it slowly penetrated her blank exhaustion that she liked it—how warm it was.

She hadn't really *liked* the way something felt in a long time.

Drying herself off slowly, she almost liked the way the towel felt, too—and yet it almost hurt. As if all her skin had been exposed to too much sun. It took that wearily acquired skill at putting one damn foot in front of the other, of continuing to survive, to get her back into the empty living area. The artfully arranged open space allowed everyone, even those in the kitchen, to enjoy the view through the great window down into the valley. Except there was no "everyone". It was a space made for people to share, but she never shared it. The whole point of moving here had been to shut herself away from any and all human hurt again. To protect her both from suffering herself and from inflicting that suffering on others.

Kai moved through the empty house as carefully as if she was climbing out of bed for the first time after a week of the flu. At the great window, she wrapped her arms around herself, staring down into the valley of humanity so far away—and started violently at the sight of Kurt's car still in the drive.

He hadn't left?

Oh—she tightened her arms around herself, flushing and vulnerable in a way she hadn't been even after the very first time they made love, years ago, when she had felt not so much vulnerable as filled with joyful confidence in him, in her body, in everything about them.

But—but where was he?

She searched him all through the house, tension growing in her as if she was looking for the monster in a horror film. Poor Kurt. He deserved so much better than the role into which time had thrust him, in her life.

She passed his jacket on the coat rack by the front door twice before she finally pulled open that door, to find him sitting on the steps, his forearms braced on his knees, his fingers locked together between them. He wore only his light cotton shirt over a T-shirt, in weather well below freezing, but he wasn't shivering.

He just sat there, staring down at his locked hands.

She grabbed his jacket to put it around him, and he gave her a startled look, not moving to take it. She pressed it back around his shoulders as it started to slide off him, sitting down beside him. "Kurt, you're freezing." As the cold started to bite through her wet hair and sweater, she realized she didn't have a jacket either.

"Am I?" he asked numbly.

"Kurt."

"I'm sorry," he said, low but still with that even, controlled diction of his, the man who could never quite mutter. "I couldn't manage to leave." He looked from his hands to her and back again. "I miss you so goddamned bad," he said helplessly and lifted his interlocked fists to press his forehead into them.

Emotion swept over her and she had to speak before it could take her, before she could drown in it. "Have you been out here all this time?" All the time she had wept, all her time in the shower, out here, in that thin shirt? "You're hypothermic," she decided, although what did she know? When she had taken that first aid class the first pregnancy—the way she had signed up for birthing classes right off the bat, and started painting the room, and called every single friend and member of their family as soon as the blue line showed up on her pregnancy test, in thrilled delight at the happy future stretching out before them—she had been focused on things like what to do if a baby choked. Like she would get a chance to *save* her child. But—an hour or more outside, in this cold? And he wasn't shivering? "Kurt, come inside. You can't drive until you've at least had a hot shower."

"If I get near a hot shower in your company, I don't know what I might do," he told his fists, a driven, desperate voice.

Ah. Everything inside her just *yanked* at the thought of what he might do, in terror and longing.

"Just come inside." She pulled at him. Whatever he did, she would have to handle it. Whatever he did— God, hadn't she handled worse?

Hadn't she *done* worse? In the end, that had been the very hardest thing to handle of all, as she pulled herself slowly into peace again, the fact that she had destroyed them in her grief and rage and a shutting-off-of-hope so intense and so crazy that only a long time later, when her hormones started to rebalance, had she realized she must have been in the equivalent of a severe postpartum depression.

He'd told her, of course. He'd tried and tried to make her go get help. She had hated him so damn much every time he said, *It's not that bad, Kai, it's okay, we've still got you and me, you're just not seeing that in the end this is just a minor thing.*

A minor thing.

A *minor* thing.

He'd tried to recoup, tried to explain that he wasn't trying to diminish her grief—*her* grief—that *minor* wasn't what he really meant, that he was just trying to say that sticking together was more important than anything else, but she just couldn't get past it—*her* grief and her rage. She couldn't get past anything he did or said or tried. She hated him for all of it.

Honey, I think there's something wrong with you.

And she had screamed, *I know there's something wrong with me! Why is it me? Why is it me? Maybe it's* you! *Maybe it's your damn sperm that don't work!*

No, Kai, I meant—honey, I know you're sad. But this isn't like you. *I think you need help.*

I'm sad? You don't even fucking care, do you? You're *not sad!*

Kai. Kai, please. Listen *to yourself.*

And she would slap her hands over her ears and run off crying, slamming doors, locking them.

He was so right. It hadn't been like her. Hadn't been like the woman he had married who always made him laugh, who used to make his face light up just by walking in the room, as if all his serious care dissolved into joy just to see her.

She had become another person and destroyed everything close to her in the transformation. As the closest and the most important, he had taken the greatest harm of all.

He scrubbed his face and looked at her over his fists warily, as if he wasn't any more sure he could stand this than she was. She grabbed one of those fists, and his hand was cold as ice. "Kurt, come *on.*" She pulled him with all her strength, and he let her drag him through the house. The luxury style cabin featured a master bathroom with a great whirlpool bath, a view out over the valley, and a shower where she could turn on sprays all up and down the wall. His mother's interior design was, of course, perfect. The quintessential luxury mountain look to which everyone should aspire.

Kai turned on the sprays, leaving Kurt to undress himself, but his fingers were too stiff, and he leaned back against the glass shower wall in defeat. Outside, through another of those great glass windows the cabin had in such plenty, the leaden afternoon was darkening further into night, and still only a few flakes of actual snow had fallen. Anger flicked suddenly through her, against Anne and her team to have been so pathetic as to let the threat of it scare them away and trap her and Kurt in this painful re-opening of wounds.

It would have been easier to undress a complete stranger and put him under the shower to save him from hypothermia than it was to strip her own former— well, in spirit former, despite the continued legal ties— husband. But she did it. Moving as fast as she could, while he stared down at her, motionless as more and more of his body was exposed. Yes, he *was* even harder, that rangy build of his pushed even more this past year until it left ripples of muscle on his abs. She could imagine him driving himself into utter physical exhaustion, evening after evening, rather than coming home to the house she had left empty.

The spray blasted against the shower wall behind him. She pushed at his jeans, her hands slipping inside them for purchase, grazing over his butt.

He was starting to shiver now, his skin icy to her touch. "Kurt, damn it. You should have come back inside. Or gotten in your car."

"I was thinking," he said. And God knew, he could think. He thought too much with that brilliant brain, sometimes, sank so deep into the problem about which he was thinking that he couldn't get out.

She had always loved it. It had made her feel protective. As if she needed to take care of that brain of his, teach him the joys of sometimes just not thinking, of just wallowing in scents and tastes and textures and the laughter of the moment.

She got the jeans and briefs off, forcing them down those long legs. He had been running a lot, hadn't he? The hard muscles of his thighs felt so good under her fingers, and it had been so long since she had touched them and—she couldn't think about that.

She pushed him back into the shower, watching him flinch as the warm sprays hit him all over, and then he shivered into the water voluptuously, his face turning up, his body slowly unfurling from a tense knot of cold as the warmth sank into his muscles.

Muscles.

Water running over skin, tracing the strength and definition of shoulders, arms, chest, abs. Water relaxing every single one of those muscles, caressing him as no one else had caressed him for so long. It trailed down over his ribs, following a V of hair down, down. As soon as the first wash of water ran over his penis, it sprang up hard again, as if only the cold had kept it contained.

She wanted to run her hands everywhere the water ran, show that damn shower how to really warm Kurt up. That water had no idea what it was doing, and she—oh, she knew exactly what Kurt liked. How hard, how fast, how long. What kind of kisses drove him a little crazy, what she could do to him if she took her hand and rubbed firm but slow, slow, slow, down from his chest, over his abs, to—

She looked back up at his face to find him watching her.

Their eyes locked through the streaming water. Her heart beat very hard.

"Kai," he said and leaned both forearms against the glass, looming over her while that clear pane kept them separate. Her heart seemed to thud in slow motion, that separation stretching out for all eternity, as if the glass would stay there forever, leaving two souls caught in longing. She wanted to go up on her tiptoes and kiss that glass, right where his mouth would meet hers.

She placed her hands against his forearms, through the pane, her own weight swaying onto them.

"Kai," he said again, a question or a demand. Or just a statement of her existence right there, on the other side of the glass.

Eyes caught by his hazel—how she loved their secret color, those sweet, gorgeous eyes that had always been *hers*—she swayed onto her toes, her lips almost brushing the glass.

He reached around the glass, grabbed her wrist, and yanked her into the shower.

Water hit her, pounding into her face, soaking her clothes, her shoes. Kurt never did that—he was never careless, and only rough in the deepest throes of lovemaking, and even that, only after he had learned that sometimes she loved it when he was rough.

Yet now, he didn't seem to give a damn that he had just ruined her shoes, that her clothes clung awkward and heavy to her. Catching her face between his hands, he lifted it up to him and kissed her, driving, hungry, starved, while the water sprayed all over them, streaming down their faces, spilling over their lips.

He kissed her until he was shaking with it, until she had forgotten they had ever stopped kissing in their lives, and yet the embrace felt as new and as compelling as that very first kiss, that day in the summer glade when the other hikers had been all that stopped them.

"God, I wish I knew what to do," he said into her throat, as her face fell back into the stream of water. He had done this before, tried to make love to her as their relationship tore apart, tried to get through to her with sex. Oh, God, they couldn't go back there again. They had been *at peace.* They had been *healing.*

And yet she didn't feel as she had then—angry and grieving and hating him—but alive, flooding with warmth, wanting to expand into him the way he had expanded into the hot water. Her hands scrubbed down his body. Those water-slickened muscles felt *so good*.

I love you.

God, where had *that* come from? She couldn't *say* that. It would do untold damage. She bit the words back as hard as she could, bit her tongue on them, and twisted her head around suddenly and bit *him*, right in the curve of his shoulder.

He drew a hoarse breath and lifted her up, pressing her back against the shower wall, so that the sprays massaged from too close, almost painful against her body. He rode her on his thigh while he pulled her soaked sweater over her head. It felt so good to have its clinging wetness off, to have the water beating painfully against her from all sides, to have his hands slide down her ribs and up again over her breasts, as warm now as the water but so much more intimate and caressing. She loved it when his hands got a little too hard on her body, when he lost his care. She had always loved that.

That old thrill of driving him crazy surged back in her as she pulled herself into him, as she found his mouth through the water and kissed it again, claiming it this time for herself, in hot, hungry, invasive kisses, taking it for hers.

He drew one of her legs up, knee bent, past his hip, stretching all her muscles, running his hand down her jeans-clad calf until he could find her furry suede slipper-boot, and he pulled it off and threw it out of the shower. Scooping that arm around her bottom to hold her into him, he pulled the other leg up and did the same thing.

Her feet, bared twice now in only an hour, and for the same reason, curled and flexed into the water, thrilled beyond measure. This warmth from him was so *gorgeous*. She wanted to soak it up everywhere.

He unfastened her jeans and worked them and her panties off her, with some difficulty, the wet denim clinging to every inch of skin on the way down. She liked it, she liked it so much, the feel of his hands loosening that denim over and over, sliding between it and skin, the water streaming down her bared legs, chasing his hands.

He knelt before her a second, when he had finally gotten them off, staring up at her. And then he surged to his feet, pressing her in one great rush of his body back into the wall, burying his face in her neck and shoulder, kissing her, nibbling her, devouring her, and then he surged up higher, until her face was the one buried in him, as he pulled her legs around his hips and cupped one hand under her bottom—and thrust into her.

He gasped when he did it. She didn't, she just wrapped her body around him, closing all her muscles on him, more than ready. Tension ran all through him, a corded, angry, desperate energy. "Kai," he said, as if he had to double-check. As if someone else might have snuck in and taken her place while he wasn't looking. Or as if he had woken time and again to find himself making love to a succubus of her. Or a dream.

She'd done that sometimes, after a summer day spent hiking in the open air, focusing on trees and birds and sky and life, trying to become again someone with whom she could live the rest of her life. She would sleep well those nights and dream of old happy days, of making love outside in the grass, and wake to find herself cuddling a pillow to her, thinking it was him.

She'd even learned to come to peace with waking that way: to stroke the pillow, kiss it, set it aside, and rise to try to learn to embrace her day again.

"Kurt." Her hands clutched him, loving how much harder it was to press into his muscle and bone than into any pillow. Loving his body's resilience, its aliveness, and how very well she knew it. "Kurt."

"Kai." He pulled almost out and thrust into her again, sinking one hand into her hair, kissing her hard, too hard, while the water poured over them. "Oh, God damn it."

Yes. Yes. God *damn* it, *damn* her, for everything.

She sank her fingers into him harder, made him real. Wrapping around him, pulling him in. *Yes, you're real, you're real, you're real. Harder. You're so real.*

Oh, this feels so good.

The thrust of him, the life, the hunger.

Don't stop, don't stop, don't stop.

But his thrusts grew too hard, too urgent, too fast to last. He forgot all about her. Taking her so fiercely, so intensely, unable to think about anything but taking.

He forgot all about her, and she didn't even mind. Wrapping her arms and legs around him as he took her, holding onto him as tightly as she could, she gloried in it. She wouldn't have let him go for anything.

Chapter 3

Afterward, both were very quiet. He handed her another towel as he dried himself, little married familiarities in the bathroom that seemed natural only in the way a great ballet was natural, such perfect, floating gracefulness in the dancers leaping around each other, and yet the slightest stumble revealed how many years of practice and work it had taken to reach that harmony.

Outside the snow had finally started to fall, soft, great flakes like feathers, insanely large and beautiful. She stepped out onto the deck outside the bathroom and stood looking up at them as they floated down onto her face to cling and melt. Kurt stood in the doorway for a moment watching her. Then he withdrew into the house.

When she found him again, he was standing looking down at the granite island, still a mess of sugar smudges from her body. She stopped in the archway, flushing. He studied her over that messy counter and then left the kitchen area for the couch that faced the window. His head disappeared from view, as if he had stretched out, and after a moment of trying to ignore the island, she finally cleaned it off, scrubbing at sugar, and then set about slicing onions and pulling broccoli out of the freezer, setting a simple soup going. A thread of pleasure twined through all the gestures, at the thought of him eating it. She had always liked to feed him.

Did they really have to talk? Could they not just move around each other in a silent truce until the roads cleared? Reluctantly, she left the pot simmering and came into the main living area, only to discover him fast asleep on the couch.

She had discovered that long body just that way

any number of times during their lives together, fallen asleep in front of a film or on a lazy Sunday afternoon after a hard game. Kurt wasn't a man who allowed himself much laziness. He was far more likely to mow the grass after a hard game than kick back and relax. She had been the one to teach him that she loved him still when he took a break. Sometimes, when she stopped to caress his sleep-softened face or pull a cover over him if it was chilly, his eyes would open, and he would smile, slow and sleepy and happy, and pull her down on top of him.

Oh, God.

Well, he had warned her. He had warned her of what might happen if they got near a hot shower together. She had known from the start that it might be more than she could handle.

But God, he was so gorgeous. She supposed he wasn't gorgeous to everyone—she had had one friend who was always falling for dramatic, black-haired Latin lovers, and another who always went for the muscled blond—but he always had been so utterly perfect to her. She loved those high cheekbones of his, the slight hollow to his cheeks that made him so photogenic, the so-average light brown hair that combined with his reserve and a heritage of excessive perfectionism to make him never realize exactly how cute he was. She loved the way his face was so lean and controlled; even in his sleep it seemed controlled, just a trick of his bone structure. And she loved that his lashes were so long, this secret hint at a world of sensitivity and passion under that reserve. She'd been so lucky that no fun-loving girl had ever thought to take him on a hike before she did.

She'd always known it was luck. That it was her sense of fun that had drawn him, and that there were a million other fun-loving girls out there, and it was just her good fortune that she had met him first.

The lamp at his head glowed over his body. He shifted slightly in his sleep, light catching on the finger of a hand loosely folded across his chest, and shock ran through her. He was wearing his wedding ring. There, a band of plain white gold on his finger, just like always. His hands, up until then, had been in his pockets, or locked around each other—or cupping her breasts— and she hadn't seen it. Or she surely had, but the ring was such a familiar part of his hand that she hadn't even noticed it before.

She had locked her own wedding rings away last spring, when the sun had started to come out after the long winter and she had slowly woken to the realization that in her grief she had destroyed the one beautiful thing in her life that she did have the power to cherish and protect, and that unlike all her other losses, *she* was the only one who had taken that power away from herself. She had bowed over the locked jewelry case and wept and wept.

But slowly, over the summer, into the fall, she had found peace. Some kind of wholeness. Something. She had packed those tears down inside her and dulled them to some temperature below zero, so that they didn't spurt up out of her and break her apart so easily anymore. She had not known exactly how she was going to be able to stand another Christmas, but she had been sure she would manage it somehow. Maybe by a sudden trip to Peru to climb to Machu Picchu. Maybe something like that.

She so did not know what to do with this. What good could come of cutting up their peace, for either of them? He had been hurt more than enough by her.

But after a moment, she pulled the throw on the back of the couch down over him and spread it out to cover him shoulders to toes. He barely shifted in his sleep, a faint smile flickering across his mouth as the luxurious softness settled over him. She wanted to kiss that smile, but she didn't. She bit her lip and straightened.

A man with a four-wheel drive could still handle this snow easily, but she didn't wake him up to send him on his way before it got worse. She went back into the kitchen and made hot chocolate.

While the soup simmered, she decided soup probably wasn't enough food for a man who had had a brush with hypothermia, so she pulled out ingredients and put together elaborate panini, the way they had often liked to do, raiding the refrigerator to come up with something new and fun. He hadn't had any experience of cooking spontaneously before he met her, and once he learned how much he could play with his food—that it was all a game and there wasn't really anything he could get wrong—he had loved it. He'd come up with the craziest flavor pairings, some of them disastrously bad, but they had just laughed.

She set the sandwiches aside to press into panini last-minute, so they would be hot, and, as the snow continued to fall and he continued to sleep, did really the best thing a woman swirling lost and looking for grounding could possibly do in those circumstances: she made chocolate chip cookies.

* * *

So Kurt woke with a smile, as he hadn't in so long he couldn't remember. Scent twined around his nose and curled into his body on each breath, teasing the corners of his lips upward. He sat up smiling, convinced he was still dreaming. One of those good dreams out of which he never wanted to wake, where it was Christmas again but back before they had ever started the devastating idea of babies, and Kai was happy with him, just with him, that way she used to be, as if he made her world as right as she made his.

Oh, he liked this dream. This was a gorgeous version of it. Those great flakes falling outside the window turned the whole dream beautiful, and it smelled so good, like love, like Kai always used to make his life smell—something savory and simmering that had onions and herbs in it, and something sweet and buttery and—was that chocolate?—to go after it.

He had been making love in this dream, too. He could feel it, which was kind of funny, really—now his dreams were getting so optimistic that he could actually feel their after-effects in his muscles—and his brain tripped over the realization that he was thinking far too much for a man still asleep, and he blinked, confused, and then pressed his face into his arm against the soft, plush back of the couch, trying not to be awake for just a little longer.

But he could hear her moving around in the kitchen, sinking the reality of this moment into him further. Every little clink of spoon against dish or thump of knife against cutting board ran jaggedly across his nerve endings, lifting the hair on the back of his neck from how scary the warmth of the sounds were. He pressed his face harder into his arm, suffocating himself in the couch.

Oh, shit, what was she going to say to him and how much was it going to hurt?

Chapter 4

Kai had cleaned the counter of all that sugar, turning it back to gleaming slick black, and Kurt couldn't decide how he felt about that. But he couldn't decide how he felt about most things right now. His insides just clenched inside him in a tight knot, afraid to feel.

He slipped his hands into his pockets, stopping in the arch that defined the kitchen space as kitchen and not living room. She gave him a fleeting, shy half-smile and focused on pulling out the heavy cast iron panini press. His mother's own brand, specially made for her in France in the enamel colors of her specifications and sold under her name by one of the major department stores. He wished Kai had chosen her own space to hide in, instead of one created by his mother, but he didn't really know what to do about it. As he didn't know what to do about pretty much anything anymore. Anyway, on the list of things he wished were different, his mother's stamp on this place was so far down in importance.

Kai set the sandwiches she had made into the press, and his heart tightened still more as he watched her, his throat clogging. She used to cook for him all the time. It had been so different from her attention to every last grain of detail when she was setting up shots or trying to create something beautiful. When she cooked for him, it had been just this relaxed, happy cooking. As if she was trying to feed something beautiful that was already there, not invent it from scratch.

It had made him feel as if some of the beauty in their life together came from him. And that she wanted to nurture that.

Another glance from her. He hadn't even known

what a shy smile looked like on her face until just now. Oh, maybe there had been a little shyness in her playful glances sometimes early on, but even then— from the first moment he had shown he was attracted to her, that first meeting, she had gazed up at him with her eyes lighting openly, no games, no reservations, as if she was entirely happy to reciprocate. He'd liked it so much. He'd tried to be *so careful* not to screw it up. Years into their marriage, on anniversaries, she would tease him about how carefully he had proceeded. He had been so determined to get everything exactly right and not ruin that spontaneous, delighted pleasure in that brown gaze when she looked up at him.

She'd always said that she had liked it a lot, that care. She'd told him once it was like a courtship. Which had made him feel centuries out of date and completely unfitted to society, but she insisted it was what had won her over for good. Sometimes—when he was feeling kind of awkward and embarrassed about the whole damn conversation and wondering if his pursuit of her had, in fact, seemed a little ridiculous to someone as laughing and easy as she was—she would even pounce on him and pretend to pin his hands to the bed and growl into his ear that the way he had courted her had been *hot*, he was so *hot*, and she would giggle and play, and—

Fuck, but he missed those days.

"That smells good," he tried, and then wished he had cleared his throat first, because his voice sounded as if it had been dragged out of bed three hours early. His fingers curled in his pockets as he waited to see if she would actually answer him this time, unlike all those attempts at conversation from the window earlier while she focused on her hush of snow, shutting him out, until finally he just—had to try something different.

She gave him another quick, shy smile. Oh, boy. That shyness was going to take some getting used to. He didn't think he objected to it exactly, though,

36

anymore than a man dreaming of summer would object to the first tiny hint of a crocus peeking through the snow.

He did clear his throat this time. "You know, it's okay if you talk." He hoped. Some of the things she had said last year, before he gave up and stopped trying to fight her need to get rid of him, had been—hard to survive.

"Is it?" she said, low, and his fingers curled in his pockets again. Because if she realized how much harm her words had done, that was, in its way, a hopeful sign, too.

"It is," he said. "At least—I hope I can take it." He tried his own half-smile back. *Please don't start telling me how much I didn't care again, or that maybe it was my sperm that were screwed up, or*—His hands tightened into fists in his pockets, bracing. He knew he had to handle it, if she did, but—*Just please don't.*

She pressed the heavy iron lid down on the panini and snuck another glance at him, this time at his— penis? No, probably his pockets. God, hope sprung eternal, didn't it? "Why are you wearing your wedding ring?" she asked suddenly, in a low rush.

His hands fisted so hard. "Because I'm married," he said. And then, out of nowhere, that anger at her, that he tried not to feel, but sometimes it lashed him mercilessly: "Or I'm sorry—did you think I was just screwing around?"

She ran a hand over her face—her *ringless hand*— and then pushed it back over her hair. She had left her hair loose after their shower, and it was nearly dry now around her face. Any minute now, the hair around her face while she worked would start driving her crazy, and she would catch it up in a ponytail. The exact same bouncy blond ponytail she had always had when she was happy. He was relieved she hadn't cut off her hair amid all the other desperate destructive gestures she had made—although he would far rather she had sacrificed her hair than him—but still . . . the ponytail was deceptive. "I don't know what to think," she said.

Really? Well, for once in the past two years, that was two of them. He tried not to find hope in that, too, but he found himself leaning forward against the counter. His whole damn body yearning toward her. "Why aren't you wearing yours?"

Because you were working with food and didn't want the rings to get gunky. Say it's that. Say it's that, Kai, don't—

"Because I left you," she said blankly, and at the same time as the words drove into his gut so violently he thought he would be sick, her eyes sparked with tears. *Good God.* Her throat had tightened over the words. *She regretted it.* She regretted leaving him.

And that he should be so grateful for that swept rage back through him, that rage that knew no reason, that just wanted to be furious at her no matter how much he forgave her. "I noticed," he said, too tightly.

"You—you sold the house," she said slowly. "I thought you had accepted that we were—through." Her breath hitched. She was trying very hard not to cry.

Oh, *fuck*, had he gotten that wrong, too? Sometimes he just wanted to *break something.* That damned glass window over there could be a start. Bash it and bash it into shards of glass everywhere that hurt everyone half as much as she had hurt him. "I couldn't live there anymore, Kai. Not afte—I couldn't. And maintaining three separate residences would have been a bit of a financial stretch for us. Mother said you weren't doing much work there for a while, so I knew you could use the money from the sale." Actually, being his mother, Anne had said, in cool, clipped tones, *And what work she is doing is quite inferior; if she doesn't pull herself together soon, I'm going to have to stop using her.* But no need to share that. Kai had pulled herself together after a few months, where work was concerned, anyway. His mother had restored her quite chary seal of approval. "And—I didn't think you would ever want to go back there again."

Besides, what the fuck was he supposed to do with the baby room? Paint it over? Leave it for her to make peace with? Stand there and stare at it every night himself without even anybody to hold on to and help him bear it? In the end he had just sold the house and given all the baby things to charity, and then he had read in those damn grief and miscarriage books that he probably wasn't supposed to have done that either.

"Oh." She stood there staring at him, her eyebrows drawn together and her lips parted, as if he had just tumbled her whole world around. They had tumbled each other's worlds around quite a few times since they had met, and he sure as hell hoped this tumble would be better than the last.

Because some of their tumbles had been bright, giddy tumbles, like wrestling in the summer grass and finding a pretty, laughing woman sitting astride you suddenly, trying to hold your arms down. But that last tumble had been more like falling off a Himalayan mountain face when you were about twenty thousand feet up, falling and falling with no hope of survival, and landing at last only to look up and see the avalanche bearing down next.

And he didn't want to think about that. God, no. He so wanted this next tumble to be a different kind. Maybe not laughter-in-the-grass, maybe he couldn't hope for that, but something warmer and softer than that avalanche, please God. Rolling over her on a rug by the fire, gentle and quiet. How about that? With a Christmas tree nearby, the room lit only by its lights and the flames. Would she let him put up a Christmas tree? If it wouldn't make her cry, that kind of tumble would work for him.

"That smells really good," he tried again. Because— her feeding of him had always been a beautiful, warm moment in their lives. It was the kind of thing a man might fall back on, in a crisis.

She blinked. "You must be hungry," she realized, with considerable relief. As if it was something she could fall back on, too.

And so, for the first time in a year and a half, she fed him. She sat down across from him and ate with him, too, a nice, rich, filling broccoli soup that was so much more vegetables than he had bothered to cook for himself the past year, and as such made him feel like— hell, like somebody cared if he lived healthily—and a sandwich, and, oh, God, cookies, her cookies.

So that was nice. So nice. In its wary, cautious, *please-don't-break-me* way. Quiet, because she seemed afraid to talk and so was he, but really, really nice. So nice that his throat clogged with it, and he had to concentrate on how to breathe. He kept discovering he was running out of oxygen because he had been afraid too deep a breath might shatter everything.

But it didn't shatter. In fact, every time he breathed, the two of them together seemed to get a little warmer, a little more real. After they ate, he found the hot chocolate she had forgotten, still heating on the stove, and poured them two cups, drawing her down on the couch to watch the snow in the night.

She tried to stir when he settled his arm over her shoulders. "Kurt, I don't think this is a good idea."

Oh, because you think I think it's a good idea? It's suicidal. But he said, "I don't mean to be rude, Kai, but it's way the fuck better than your last one."

Which was probably the wrong thing to say on his part, too, but she shut up, and they sipped hot chocolate and watched the snow. He hadn't really meant to shut her up; he was pretty sure he would like for her to talk to him, if she was in a place where she could talk without screaming again. But—her body felt so damn warm against his. Why risk it moving away?

He let it soak into him, the warmth of her, the scent of her hair, like rain at last on parched earth. *Oh, thank God, thank God, thank God . . .*

And underneath the relief, the soul of a grown man who wanted to curl himself into a fetal ball in a dark place and whimper as torturers grabbed at him and hauled him away: *Oh, God, please don't let it hurt as much as last time.*

Chapter 5

K ai woke happy and feeling loved, and she hadn't in a long time. Contented, yes, she had managed that. Able to stand on her own two feet. Able to live alone, be alone, be strong—all those things, she had reached, slowly, starting maybe last spring, or maybe even the grieving process over the winter had been part of it.

But happy—loved—she had kind of forgotten she could feel that way. She knew she didn't *deserve* to feel that way, and so now—to wake up warm on a couch, with a chest shifting under her face and an arm wrapped around her—it made tears fill her eyes. Warm tears, the tears she had tried so hard to freeze. Those tears blurred the snow still lazily, gently falling through the window as the sky lightened, as if the snow wasn't quite ready to yield itself to sun just yet.

The tears spilled over, running silently down her cheeks and plopping onto his shirt. She hadn't thought he was awake, but one hand came up to stroke her hair. He didn't speak, and neither did she.

Finally she had to sniffle so badly that she pulled herself off the couch and went in search of a tissue. His hand fell away from her departing back reluctantly, but he didn't try to catch hold of her. She stood in front of the bathroom sink staring at herself and that made her cry again, for this person in the mirror who used to have so much and who had destroyed all of it. She sat on the closed toilet with her head in her hands and cried and cried.

She had worked so hard to be done with tears like this. And yet their onslaught was almost comforting. *Oh, there you are. I've missed you. I guess we're not done with each other after all.* She had had to learn how to do things like that, once the pregnancies started failing—learn how to cry inconsolably, learn how to be angry, learn how to recover. She had done a shit hell job of all of them, she supposed, and she was sorry, she was so sorry, but that, too, she had had to learn how to deal with—her guilt and regret and that great grief that was her marriage. That was him.

When she finally cleaned herself up—matter-of-factly, used to this—and came back downstairs, Kurt was asleep again, curled into the back of the couch with the blanket pulled over his head like a willful child, refusing to wake up. It surprised her. Kurt had always woken too easily, bordering on insomniac, as if he found it too troubling to lay his carefulness and control aside and had to pick them back up again as fast as possible. He had *always* been the first one out of bed in the morning.

She gazed at the long form under the blanket and finally shook her head and went into the kitchen. But there, instead of the Greek yogurt that she usually ate for breakfast these days, for efficient, palatable nourishment, she paused, and rolled her shoulders—and then she smiled suddenly, her whole heart lifting with pleasure at this morning, as she started to pull out ingredients.

As if the tears or maybe the touch of Kurt's lips had washed away some ugly, jagged splinter blocking her heart.

She made waffles and sprinkled them with powdered sugar, blushing a little bit as she sifted it over the golden waffle. One of the strawberries she cut in half looked exactly like a heart, and she set it in the center of Kurt's waffle, sifting a little more powdered sugar over it—and then blushed again and whisked the heart away, looking up to find him standing in the archway watching her. Behind him, the sun was starting to break through clouds and limned him in a softly diffused light.

"That smells really good," he said, heartfelt, just as he had the night before, and she felt her face brighten into something it hadn't felt in a long time—laughter.

"Poor man, has no one been feeding you?" she teased, and then caught herself, on the edge of the teasing, because there were so many parts to that which weren't funny at all. She didn't have the right to laugh with him anymore.

But his eyes snagged on her face for a long moment, and he came forward to the island so that the nimbus around him softened and she could see his smile. Not the smile he had when she made him laugh, but the smile he had always had when she just made him happy. When he was just glad to look at her. "No," he said quietly.

Tears threatened again abruptly. How could he smile at her? It made her so sad to think of him going for a year and a half without anyone feeding him. Damn it, he deserved so much *better* than what he had gotten. And she just couldn't give that better anymore.

She bent her head and stared at the golden waffle, under the weight of what she had done to that happiness. "I'm sorry," she whispered to the spot in the middle of the waffle where the little strawberry heart had been.

He reached across the wide island, a stretch even for him, and closed his hand around hers. His wedding band glowed simple and strong. "I'm glad. I always hoped you would feel sorry one day."

Her mouth twisted. That was—fair, she supposed, that he would want her to regret it. What was she supposed to make of this touch, of this strange, snow-kissed togetherness after all this time? The pieces of them had been shattered and scattered so completely, how was she supposed to put them back together again? Why would he let her even try?

Her try? She was afraid to even leave a heart strawberry in the middle of his waffle.

He was the one trying. She wasn't even sure what he was trying to do exactly, except perhaps reach a point of forgiveness. And if so, she had been right: forgiveness really hurt.

But she could stand hurt, couldn't she? She had proven that.

Maybe she should stand a few things again, for his sake.

So, on a sudden burst of determination, she sliced up more strawberries into fine hearts to layer all over his waffle, a whole mad field of hearts, and sprinkled it with sugar—and added whipped cream, hell, why not?—and stuck one last strawberry-heart in the mad Seussian mountain of cream, as if the Grinch's heart had popped out of him when it grew three sizes too big—and slid it across to him.

He had sat on a stool at the edge of the island by then, watching her, and when the plate slid to a stop in front of him, he actually grinned.

Grinned. She hadn't seen him grin in—what, two years? He hadn't grinned during the last six months of their marriage.

"You know, you had me at the waffle," he told her, and the urge to grin back at him struggled with the fear that she didn't have the right to. What had she been doing, savoring happiness this morning while he slept? When had she gotten the nerve to feel *happy*?

He picked up the strawberry heart tucked on top of the cream and pressed a kiss to it, his eyes closing. Then he ate it in one hungry snatch, like a wolf might down a scrap before anyone else could wrench it from him.

She found herself blushing, a tendency that was new. She had never really blushed much with him, simply because from the very first, he had always made her feel so sure and happy. She had destroyed that surety, though, willfully and wantonly, and it had taken some doing. He had been as sure for her as any man could possibly be.

Her eyes prickled again, and she focused on her

own waffle, no fancy strawberries on it, just a dusting of powdered sugar. Out of the corner of her eye, she caught his finger tracing around the edge of his plate. When he brought it to his mouth and sucked the sugar off it, she blushed all over.

And peeked to find him watching her, transfixed, finger still in his mouth.

He stretched across the island to pull her plate to the stool right beside him and then, as she came after it, ridiculously shy, he took one of his own strawberry hearts and placed it neatly in the center of her waffle. That stopped her dead just before she climbed onto the stool, tears threatening again.

He kissed her, hoisting her up onto the stool himself, and slipped her a fork. His hand rested a moment over hers, that warmth that only yesterday she had never thought to feel again. "This tastes so damn good, Kai," he said softly. "You have no idea."

"You haven't even tasted the waffle yet." His manners bound him to wait until they both were served.

He grinned again. "You had me at the strawberry," he said this time and touched a bit of whipped cream to her nose. An unheard-of silliness from Kurt. It was more like something she would once have done.

He swooped in and kissed the cream off her nose and sat back to dig into his waffle. The amount of happiness suddenly shimmering off him was too much for her to process. Didn't he remember that their happiness was all gone?

He closed his eyes on the first bite of waffle in pure bliss and opened them to catch her staring. He smiled.

It had once seemed so normal, to construct happiness out of flour, butter, eggs, and strawberries and to bake it into something golden and sweet for a morning. Now it seemed incredible—such a fragile joy in the face of all the great destructive grief that could tear through that moment and destroy it.

At one point, grief and anger had pushed her so far over the edge that she would have destroyed this moment herself, on the grounds that all that happiness and hope was false. But now—it wasn't really that she believed in those flowers sprouting out of the snow, as she used to. But she knew better than to stomp on them and grind them into the mud just so nothing else could grind them first.

So they ate their waffles, every bite an unbelievable burst of golden *flavor*. She couldn't remember the last time she had *tasted*. He cleaned every last crumb from his plate. She ate around her little strawberry heart, until it stood bereft on an island of powdered gold. It felt too wrong for *her* to eat that heart, like giving the prince's heart to the wicked witch instead of to the happy, singing princess.

Kurt's fork speared through heart and waffle both, and he slipped the whole bite into her mouth. Then, while she was still trying to convince herself it was okay for her to chew it, he rose briskly, taking their plates to the sink. Over the running water, he asked, "Would you like to go for a walk?"

Even when Kurt did the cooking—grilling out, maybe—he tended to wash the dishes automatically at the end of the meal. His compulsive mother had probably never allowed dirty dishes to lie around, so probably nurture had something to do with it, but his childhood household had had staff. He wouldn't have ever had to wash a dish himself, growing up. So Kai had always thought another element besides environmentally-induced obsessive-compulsiveness must contribute to how voluntarily he did any household chores that needed doing: he had an ingrained need to take care of the good things in his life, and her cooking for him was one of the good things.

"In the snow?" she asked.

His half-smile was careful, watchful. "That's right."

She had walked so much in the snow up here. But

if she added him to the excursion—she was a little afraid of snow, still. Because, well—she had just wanted so damn badly to have their own child with whom to play in it by now. Back in the good old days, she had even imagined that by this age they would have two or three kids; they would *talk* about it, God, as if this was in their control: "Three might be a lot. We would have to get a bigger house." "Three seems like an odd number. I think it should be either two or four, so one of them doesn't feel left out." "Ha, if you want four, *you* get pregnant." That retort had been back early in the first pregnancy, when she just thought it was going to be all vicious nausea but eventually with a happy ending. Or a happy beginning. Whatever you wanted to call it. "Well, don't you want at least one of each, a little girl and a little boy? I hope the little girl will look just like you." *Stupid* conversations like that.

By the third attempt, she would have been desperately happy with just one. And then, and then—she just couldn't stand to try, not ever again. God, the first baby would have been *four* this Christmas, if she had lived to be born. Her third baby had actually been due on Christmas Day. Her little miracle baby, she had thought at it in her belly, all through that spring, and tried to believe in the magic of the third try *so hard*.

Her nostrils stung, the way they did sometimes when everyone else thought she should be over it by now. It had been part of the reason that she had had to get so far away from everyone else.

She took a breath and sighed it out. "Yes, all right. Let's go for a walk."

Chapter 6

K urt focused on the hot water running over the plates, grateful for it. He had never understood it when he discovered that their friends' couples fought over such stupid things as doing dishes or mowing the grass or making sure someone's tank was filled with gas. They were all such easy things to *get right.*

It turned out they didn't count for much, when the going got tough, but it used to be, when he wasn't ever entirely sure how he had managed to convince this much sunshine to enter his life, that he found them very reassuring. Little things to keep that sunshine happy. Look at this plate, for example: it had just held the most delicious waffles and hearts for him, and now, instead of leaving it some ugly mess no one would ever want to deal with later, he was cleaning it right up, fresh and shiny and ready for a new start.

When you had a woman who was willing to cook for you, and laugh and tease you while she did it, you didn't really want to leave any barriers lying around the kitchen that would discourage her from getting in that cheerful, cooking mood again the next evening or even sometimes spontaneously for breakfast. Up until things went so wrong, he had been kind of quietly, contentedly smug about how well this philosophy worked compared to those of his idiot friends.

But then, of course, all of those friends still had their wives, and even kids, now, and complained about them, too. Told him he should be glad, that he didn't know how much trouble he had escaped.

The fucking bastards.

He drew a breath, easing his fingers on the plate before he cracked it, and set it to dry. "I'll go get my snow boots from the car." He had put snow gear into the back as he always did when driving in winter weather, just in case. Like the dishes, it used to profoundly reassure him when he was packing up Kai's snow gear, too, and a big box of energy bars, in case they got stranded—doing everything in his power to keep his wife and their world together protected and happy. Packing up just his own snow gear felt—shitty. Really, really shitty.

"All right," she said, smiling at him tentatively as he left. He was probably pushing this too soon, getting everything wrong *again*, but *God*, he did not want to spend another Christmas Day like last one. Just this grinding agony of minute after minute of a day to get through. Knowing she was by herself and that her agony must be even *worse*. And that there was nothing he could do to help; everything he did only made her misery more unbearable.

He knew why men killed themselves when they lost their families.

He just hadn't had that option, last Christmas. He knew he had to hold through and get his family back.

He hadn't even been able to drink himself into oblivion, because—well, for one thing he didn't even know how to get drunk. He'd done it once as a college student and not liked the experience *at all*. Kai had often tried to tease him into drinking an extra glass of wine, but he had always worried about what he might do if he lost control—what if it was something she would find ridiculous or offensive?

But that Christmas Day, he would have been happy to test out getting drunk again, except—what if she called? What if she just couldn't make it through that Christmas Day and needed him? He had to be able to drive.

God.

Anything would be better than that Christmas Day again.

Except, maybe, failing to make things right this time, too. What if he hit a point when he had to give up all hope?

No, don't think like that. She had smiled. She had made waffles. She had put hearts on them, which was the kind of sweet, silly thing she used to do for him. He'd had to start acting silly himself, because otherwise all the emotions that rushed up in him might have come out as, God forbid, tears. He'd cried for her once—all those words she was wielding back then breaking him like a damn rack. It had actually seemed to work—she'd softened, as if the tears had shocked through to her heart and she'd remembered that hers sometimes beat for him, too. She'd wrapped her arms around him and whispered she was sorry, she was sorry, she didn't mean it, she was so sorry—and they had made love. It had been so sweet, and he had been so *glad*, that things might finally work out, that she finally understood he did care—

And she had left him the very next day. Crying herself. "I just can't. I just can't do it anymore."

"But—Kai, why? I thought—didn't we—"

"I just can't."

God.

He pulled his snow pants and snow boots on, sitting on the edge of the bumper, zipped his ski jacket up to his chin and pulled on his gloves—nice, thick armor everywhere—and went back into the house to pull her out into this snow. Hoping it wasn't the wrong thing to do.

The way she walked on the snow at first, anyone would have thought she was a kitten seeing snow for the first time. Which broke his heart a little, but his heart was so used to being broken by then. She was the one who had taught *him* to play in the snow, before he quite understood that adults were allowed to. He still remembered how she'd done it, the sideways evil laughing look as she tested a handful of snow before she lobbed it straight at him. She had lousy aim, and he'd just smiled at her when it bounced off his shoulder, shaking his head indulgently as he kept walking. The next one had hit him square on the back, sliding harmlessly off his jacket. So she had run up to him and kissed him, and God knew, he should have expected what was coming, but it was their first snow together, and he had just sunk delightedly into his kiss, until a cold handful of snow went straight down his collar and he yelped.

After which, what was a man supposed to do? He'd *had* to get her. And it had been so much fun. He had felt like a kid again, until he caught her at last and rolled her under him in the snow, when he'd realized— no, it wasn't childish. No, he was an adult, his body at that moment felt very, very adult, and this was how his adult life could *be*, with her. Happy. Thrilled. Aroused. Zinging with energy and fun. Forever.

He'd proposed to her that night. She'd been so happy, too. As if, in offering himself to her, he had offered her the whole world.

And the forever of fun had lasted a few years. It turned out she had wanted more in her world than him, but that hadn't really been a surprise when he understood how important that was to her, or even a disappointment, just, eventually, a—regret. Because he himself was all he could actually offer her. The rest of what she wanted was even more beyond his control than hers. It wasn't even happening in *his body*; it was all in hers. And he knew that his physical distance from it was something for which she had a very hard time forgiving him.

Although he had tried to control what happened, God. He had tried everything: talking to her the first time—*We can try again, honey*—oh, *shit,* had that been a bad idea. And the second time: *Don't think about it, honey, please don't get your hopes up.* In a way, that technique had worked well for him, the second time—to just turn his brain off, not believe in it at all. Except that she had hated him so much for his ability to do that and for his attempts to get her to do it, too. And the third time—he had just lived in pure, knotted dread, so worried about her that he couldn't even stand to think about the baby at all, except as what the little fetus might do to her if it didn't, if it didn't—

And then it hadn't.

And none of his attempts to solve things, to make her better--*Maybe we should adopt,* or *Honey, we've got us at least,* or *Honey, what do you think about a little trip to the Bahamas? India? Mount Everest?*—had worked *at all.*

He looked down at her now, not really hoping for a spark of that old laughter and not finding it, either. But she settled into the walk, the kitten finally figuring out that the snow wouldn't hurt her or at least that it was a hurt she could bear, her shoulders relaxing and a little sigh running through her, her face growing thoughtful and quiet, sadness in there, yes, but a sadness with which she had made some kind of peace.

He took his glove off—stupid armor—and caught a snowflake off her lashes, then rubbed it against her cold-flushed cheek. Her face brightened, like a surprise to her, and she looked up at him. He smiled down at her. "If I drop snow down your neck, will you chase me and kiss me?"

Her lips curled cautiously up at the corners, her eyes crinkling with a hint of her old humor. That humor was so wary now, and he wanted to coax it out of hiding. *It's all right. I know your laughter got brutalized, but we're in a safe space now. Aren't we?* "You might be banned from waffles for the rest of your life," she threatened him, and then her eyes flickered.

Oh, did you realize that to ban me from waffles, you'd have to actually let me back in for the rest of my life?

"I guess I won't risk it," he said. And then he tripped her and took her down in the snow, just like that, his pulse leaping in a giddy, testosterone-laced surge to be doing something so outrageous in their current circumstances. He cushioned her fall with his arms, bracing himself over her with a grin. "Let's make a snow angel instead."

But her hint of laughter faded away, and he could see her swallow. "I can't yet," she whispered. "She would have been four."

Their first attempt at a child. Their second attempt would have been a boy of almost three, and their last attempt would have been just turning one. For a moment, visions flashed through his mind—a little blonde girl making snow angels, and a brown-haired boy throwing snowballs at her, and maybe him holding a tiny one-year-old by the hand to help her walk—and his own throat closed. He bent and kissed Kai, slow and firm, and pulled them back to their feet. "All right," he said quietly and put his arm around her shoulders as they kept walking.

They hiked a long time, up through the woods. The snow was fresh and quiet under the trees, winds in the upper branches stirring flakes down on them gently, as if they were walking under Kai's sieve of powdered sugar. He smiled at the thought of comparing the taste of sugar on her skin to that of real snow, and then his smile faded slowly as the idea grew in him, replacing pleasure in the fancy with arousal and a sense of its danger. Yes, kissing her was incredibly dangerous, more dangerous than any risk he had ever taken. He just never knew, now, how Kai might react to anything he did. That certainty of her happiness in him, once so precious, had been entirely destroyed.

Arousal and its danger laced together, strengthening each other like rival armies inciting each other to battle. The white-and-shadow quiet under the trees contrasted with the thump of his blood through his veins. A bright red cardinal flashed by like a glimpse of a broken heart, and he turned her against a pine tree and sipped a snowflake right off her cheek.

Ah—cold and fragile, yielding instantly to the warmth of his mouth and her skin. Not sweet, like her sugar, but purified of flavor.

He caught snow off the nearest branch and rubbed

a pinch of it over her cheekbone, making her gasp and shiver. He breathed an apology over that snow, melting it, and kissed the cold spot, warming her up again.

With a little sigh, she nestled her cheek against his kiss. So he rubbed more snow over her lips, and she winced from the cold and opened her mouth to protest—and he kissed her there, too, drinking the snow all away, slipping into the heat of her mouth, until cold held them in its grip everywhere except for the meeting of their mouths, their tongues, the way he took and took and took from her and tried to give back.

She liked it so much more than he expected. Even after yesterday, on her granite island and in her shower, he still didn't believe in the way she warmed to him in a rush of grateful hunger, her mouth opening and taking, her hands climbing up to press cold gloves into his neck, frustrating him beyond belief. He wanted her to just strip those gloves off and press her ice-cold fingers straight into him.

Anyone would think he would have had the good sense to do this with the snow right by her hot tub, but no, here they were, deep in the woods with no recourse against the cold all around them but each other. Their bodies, their warmth.

And lots and lots of icy snow.

Let's make it melt for us. Let's kiss it all away.

I love you, Kai. Are you ready to love me just a little again?

He pushed her up on his thigh against the tree, thrilling to the power in his hands, how easily he could handle her body compared to every other thing he had had to handle in their lives. Something visceral and animal surged through him at the power, fed by the scent of pine and the cold hush. "I could take you right here," he said, guttural.

Her hips surged up against his, still such an unexpected hunger for him that she nearly toppled them in the snow right there. "Oh, God, I love it when you *say* things like that with that perfect, perfect accent of yours," she said, petting his head frantically with her clumsy gloves and pulling herself up into him.

What? Didn't he talk like a normal person? But he couldn't check because her mouth had tangled with his, as if *she* was starved for *him.*

No, she couldn't possibly be as starved as he was. He devoured her mouth to prove it, a battle of starvations. God, all that hunger in the shower had been *nothing.* A greater hunger swamped him, as if yesterday's attack had just been some tiny signal to his body that it had the right to an appetite again. Oh, God, she tasted so—he wanted so much more—he—

"If I could take you right here—" His voice sounded harsher than the tree bark under his palms. He lowered it. "I would rub snow all over your breasts." She flinched at the thought as he cupped them through her thick jacket. His voice dropped until it was almost as soft as the hushed woods: "And then suck it all off."

She shivered, from cold or heat or maybe the battle of both.

"I think I'd even rub it here." His hand massaged into the V of her jeans, thorough and when he felt the hot hint of dampness, harder. "And then make that melt, too."

"I'd freeze," she protested, even as she climbed into him, seeking warmth against that idea of freezing, seeking it from *him.* Rubbing herself against him, oh, shit, yes, God. "Kurt, you wouldn't do that to me. I'd *freeze.*"

Maybe. His brain had exploded into that place of arousal where it didn't really matter what made sense, what might actually work. "I'd like to try it, though," he breathed, rubbing her jeans harder. Hunger and power leaped in one great glorious surge in him when her head arched back, when her body grew pliant to him. God, he loved it when he shut her brain off, shut off all her ability to take action, as if her whole self just yielded to the need to be his. He loved how the harder he got, the more he wanted to take her, the softer she got and the more she wanted to be taken.

"No," she managed to whisper, shaking her head. "No way."

"Let's get back to your hot tub." He grabbed her wrist and pulled her from the tree. "Damn it, why did we hike so far away?"

"Kurt, I swear to God, if you try to rub snow on my chacha, I am wrapping one great bit fistful of it around your dick," she told him, even as she let herself be dragged along after him. He nearly stopped dead, and it wasn't from the fistful of snow image, which, granted, was hideous—maybe that whole snow against her sex fantasy wasn't one he should actually *do*—but because she sounded—well, she sounded like the woman who had once dropped snow down his collar and dodged laughing behind trees until he caught her.

"Just wait and see if you like it first," he said soothingly, while the fact that he was *teasing* her ran through him giddily. He allowed himself the daring, long-lost privilege of a smirk at her. "You never know, you might beg for more."

She scooped up a fistful of snow and lobbed it at him.

Good *God*. She had actually done that. Just thrown a lopsided snowball at him, as if laughter and teasing had surged past these terrible years and broken out again. He grabbed his own fistful and threw it back at her in a wild burst of so much testosterone and so much hunger that he accidentally aimed it with his full competitive skill and hit her straight in the face.

Her jaw dropped in pure indignation—Kurt *never* hit her straight in the face in snowball fights, and he had a second's guilty relief that he hadn't taken the time to pack his snow into a proper snowball, before she jumped up, grabbed the branch over her head— and jerked all her weight down on it, leaping to the refuge of the trunk as snow dumped on top of him.

He burst out laughing as he shook himself, so much happiness pressing suddenly through him that it threatened to split his skin, and at the same time this dominant greediness, so that he just had to *catch* her, take her, make this moment all his.

He lunged for her so menacingly that she squeaked with alarm and dodged behind the tree, then to another tree. And then they were weaving in and out among the pines. He wanted to catch her so damn bad and yet he wanted to toy with her, too, cat and mouse, make her squeal and tremble in terror of being caught and yet want it so much she forgot everything but him.

He surged at her, growling, and she threw a fast snowball at him, too unnerved to pack and aim it properly. He let her dodge away to a refuge behind a big oak where she couldn't see his body . . . and then he stalked her around it, coming in close to the trunk, making her peek one way and another in vain, her tension ratcheting up a notch, and then another, until he lunged at her with a growl—

She screamed again, louder, freer, ever happier, and ran to the next tree, and the next, as he chased her and caught her and let her manage to wiggle free, taking his snow punishment as she tried to defend herself and then catching her again.

I love you, I love you, I love you so damn much, Kai, so much that he finally couldn't *stand* it anymore, and he tackled her in one hard lunge, taking her down and cupping her head in the snow with his bare hands to protect it as he kissed her and kissed her.

"Is that hot tub any closer yet?" he groaned, rolling them over to get her out of the snow. Christ, she was cute. She looked just like she had the day he had proposed. Except for the thinner cheeks, but *let's just not think about those things right now, sweetheart. Let's just be us, let's just be happy. I think that might be how life works, that sometimes it takes all your happiness away and you just have to build it back, bit by bit. Or some people don't build it back, but we're not going to be*

*those people. We're not going to leave our lives in ruins;
we're going to put them back together again.* He pulled
her down to him and kissed her again, and again, in no
hurry to ever let this kissing end.

In case he couldn't get it started again.

"I'm never getting so far away from a hot tub in the
winter again in my life," he swore finally, pushing them
to their feet again. "How much farther? A couple of
miles?"

"Don't worry, you'll have forgotten all about it by
then," she said soothingly, patting him on the back like
a small boy she was trying to console, with a little
smirk.

"You've forgotten the persistence of my
imagination, Kai Winters." He dusted her hair off and
pulled her hat back on her head, loving everything
about this moment—her teasing, the way she had
forgotten sorrow, even that reaffirmation of his name on
her.

She grinned. "I'll believe it when I see it," she said
saucily, taunting him with the swing of her hips as she
headed back to the trail. What a beautiful sight that
swinging butt was. She *still* hadn't remembered to be
unhappy.

"Are you sure?" he murmured menacingly, as he
came close behind her, enjoying being the hungry
threat bearing down on her. "That you'll need to see it?
Are you sure I couldn't blindfold you and still somehow
manage to convince you how long my imagination can
last, Kai?"

She darted a glance back at him over her shoulder,
her eyes brilliant with alarm, but it was a fun alarm,
she was loving every second of it, he could tell.

He caught up with her enough to grab her by the
collar and run a little dusting of snow up and down her
nape. She yelped and shivered all over, and he bent
down and growled low in her ear. Her head arched back
to him at that, her eyes closing, and he laughed, taking

her hand and falling into step beside her. Fuck, this might actually turn into a good Christmas.

Chapter 7

G od, he felt so animal, so animal, so animal, sinking her into the hot tub naked, lifting her out just enough to rub her breasts with snow while she writhed and half-fought and entirely yielded, sucking the snow off her nipples, sinking her down again, wallowing in sensations until there was nothing left of them but senses. Until they were nothing but animals. Utter animals.

He did try the snow on her sex. He'd kept her in the hot tub a long time by then, until they were both much too hot, and he laid her back on the edge of it and watched her face and watched her sex as he rubbed a finger of snow up those intimate lips. She shivered and clenched and tried to fight it, and he parted her and slipped more cold snow with his finger deep inside her. She flinched, trying to get away—but not *too* hard, oh, no, she let him hold her down, panting and panting. God, she liked it when he controlled her. It always drove him crazy, how much she liked that. He bent and took her with his mouth again, sucking all that coldness away. She winced into it so much and she melted afterward so well that he did it over and over, even testing a snow-cold thumb on her clitoris, feeling vaguely, satisfyingly cruel, utterly, evilly delicious as she flinched and melted, flinched and melted, let him conquer all cold, let him make her come.

He loved taking her in that hot tub and snow. He did all kinds of things to her in that hot tub. He hadn't thought he had so much animal in him. He hadn't known that so did *she*—melting into him, rounding into him, arching into him, wallowing in him as if she never wanted to climb out of the sensuality of it enough to let her brain turn on ever again.

He put his mouth to her and sucked her humanity

straight out of her. Made her scream. God, but he loved making her scream.

Loved the helpless, violent convulsions of her, how she became so weak and vulnerable in his hands, loved petting those out and driving her up into them again. He loved it probably past any kindness, because he drove her into exhaustion and then had to carry her to the bed.

And he took her one last time there, while she was almost asleep, just lax and willing, took her just because they were in a *bed*, a big king *marital* bed, and he wanted to make it *his* bed, *their* bed, and even though he had just come not long ago in the hot tub, the need to take her again rose up in him, too strong. He didn't care if she half-dreamed her way through it. He had taken her plenty of times in his dreams, in the past year and a half.

Her turn to let him into *her* dreams.

Exhausted with all that animal sex, she didn't seem to mind, her body still willing, easy, her arms sliding loosely over him but still holding him as he took her, her body curling into him when he was done, as they both fell asleep.

And that was the most beautiful thing of all, to sleep in a big bed together again.

He hadn't always realized this, back in the days when their future could only hold bright, happy things, but to sleep together in a bed might very well be so beautiful that if it was all the beauty his life could hold—he would still take it.

Chapter 8

Waking was sleepy, happy, and then it shocked through Kai that the long body lying so close to hers wasn't a dream, and she held herself still, heart in her throat, as if that dream might catch her and turn into a nightmare.

The potential nightmare slumbered, though, beautiful. A lithe, long, muscled body, warming all the space under the covers. He wasn't eating enough, she thought, and touched his wrist, there where the tendons were so relaxed now in sleep. Of course, he wasn't. He was probably swimming at lunch and running again in the evening, going rock climbing on weekends, playing Ultimate relentlessly—anything but sitting down at the kitchen table and . . . and—eating cold cereal by himself?

Of course he was.

Grief squeezed her again for all the hurt she had done him. But she realized she no longer wanted to shut him out of her life so that she didn't have to deal with that grief. Whether the grief had just grown more manageable with time, or whether her heart had grown stronger from all it had had to learn to bear, she did not know, but she breathed through the wave of grief quietly, letting it subside and just rest there, not trying to heal it or stop it or chase it away. Just letting it be. It was there. It would always be there. If she left it alone and did not worry at it, maybe it would take a nap.

That was one thing she had learned over time. Grief was exhausting. And sometimes even the biggest grief in the world exhausted itself, like a big, bad, ugly winter that finally, even if it was late June by then, had to lay itself down and let a few daffodils push up through its weary snow.

She stroked from his wrist up that long arm, its

strength in abeyance. Tears dampened her eyes as she imagined him as daffodils—such a funny image for his athletically geeky carefulness and controlled masculinity—and yet it suited him somehow. Stubborn, persistent, determined to get through the snow. She didn't try to do anything about the tears—not wipe them away, not hold them back—and they dried after a moment without falling, while her hand traced over his collarbone.

He really had such a beautiful form to him. It just worked for her. Not bulky, just defined and strong and lovely. She liked the bones of him. She liked that lean over-thought athleticism.

But she always had. Her fingers trailed down his torso, over too-defined ribs—he was not *eating*—loving that resilient texture of him. From the very first—when she had seen his attraction to her and the way he handled it with such care, such a determination to get her right—she had wanted to get her hands on him. He'd driven her just a tiny bit crazy with how carefully he had courted her, but she had liked it, too. It had made her want to grab him and get past that careful restraint of his. Made her long to sink her hands into him. See what he *felt* like. Both her hands curved around his ribs in that remembered need. In that still urgent need.

She flexed her hands gently, trying not to wake him as she stole a little of that warm resilience again. The ability to do that felt so good. It released tension all down her spine, and the hairs on her body shivered with it.

He was so *beautiful*. The heat of him felt as if it could soak right through to her heart. Melt it. Tears sprang up again at the thought, but maybe that was just the melting ice.

God, she hadn't realized how much ice she had inside her. She had forgotten how very, very cold everything had grown, so used to that cold that it had begun to seem just the way the world was: a severe and ugly place best suited for hibernation.

Her lips trembled upward at the corners as she traced over his hip. She still did not know if she wanted to wake up again, to come down out of those snowy clouds and be a human being again.

But he was beautiful. She could not touch him if she stayed up in the winter clouds. She could not feel that warmth at her fingertips.

Kurt's lashes lifted slowly, for an instant his eyes wary, as if he, too, was afraid of shifting from a dream into nightmare. But then he smiled at her like a deliberate choice, like those daffodils pushing their heads up through the snow, and he touched her cheek.

The moment reminded her of the morning after their wedding, when she had wakened to find him gazing at her like that, faces so close, and he had smiled, a slow blush climbing up his cheeks so that anyone would have thought he was some teenage bridegroom who had just made love for the first time.

"You don't think this will just make everything harder?" she asked low.

"No," he said quietly and fiercely. "Not trying would have been harder. Spending another Christmas like last one would have been harder."

She took a deep breath, struggling with it. Because it felt harder to her. Far, far harder than what she had been doing these past few months, trying to float above the surface of her grief and loss and just somehow find a way forward.

"But—" Watching her, he sighed and for a moment looked so tired. His hand curved around her cheek. "I can't speak for you."

"Kurt." She turned her face into his hand, hiding in its shelter. "You've, ah—" Her throat clogged. "You've always been worth me doing something hard. It just—I couldn't, I couldn't—"

His fingertips shifted gently on her forehead, his thumb against her temple. "I figured out that you couldn't. It took me a while. Until the day you walked out and I didn't chase after you, I guess. I wanted to chase after you so badly."

Her mouth twisted against the heel of his palm. "I'm sorry. Did it take you a long time to get over it?"

A short silence. And then, so carefully the air could have been crystal and any word would shatter it into shards that pierced their hearts: "The babies?"

He hadn't had *trouble* over the babies, that old lash of anger twitched her. Nothing like hers. Of course he had gotten over *them*. Her babies. "Me leaving."

Another silence. She breathed in the scent of his palm. "*Get over* isn't the right phrase."

"Move on," she said carefully. Her throat felt full of fog, and when she spoke each word seemed to puff that wintry whiteness over him. "You—know."

He left the bed abruptly, grabbing one of yesterday's abandoned towels to wrap around his waist, and went to stand by the great window. Outside, too, fog lowered over the snow, the air so thick that the tiniest blink from a snow queen's eyes would crystallize everything. His towel was white against the white past the glass, only his body, even at its winter palest, still bringing a hint of warmth, of life, to the scene. She knew those windows were double-paned, and yet his position next to that great expanse of glass seemed like a very cold place to be.

"It's funny how two people can love each other, and live together for years, and still not realize how very differently they think about things," he told the glass. His hands curled into fists and slid across his towel, failing to find pockets in which to bury themselves. "I haven't gotten over it, or moved on. It never occurred to me to try."

Against that glass and winter world, he looked so lonely she thought she would die. But that wouldn't cure anyone's loneliness problems, would it?

"I've been waiting," Kurt told the glass. Something

spasmed across the profile of his face, some violent twisting of despair, endurance, hope. He pressed his forehead against the pane until his neck corded. "Waiting very hard."

Oh, God, she couldn't even think. Feelings were swelling up too big, threatening her wholeness. And yet they seemed—stronger, different, than those old feelings that had torn her apart. Almost as if she had turned into a shrunken old balloon and they were stretching her back out again. "Waiting—for me to come back?"

She saw his throat muscles work. "God, Kai, you don't know. You don't know how many days I tried not to get through on the hope that when I walked back through the door, you would be there, telling me how sorry you were. You don't know how many days I tried not to think about that, tried not to hope for that."

Tears rushed up into her eyes. Would she *never* come to an end of crying? But she could see him. She could see him, his car slowing as he turned down the street to their house, his heart tightening. She could see him telling himself, when her car wasn't in the drive, to stop hoping, that was it, she wasn't there—and still hoping a little, nevertheless, as he got out of the car, as he turned the key in the lock. She could see him doing it a shade too slowly, trying to put off that moment when he looked into the house—and saw it was empty. Still. "I'm so sorry," she whispered.

His mouth twisted in what was maybe supposed to be a smile. "But I haven't been waiting for you to come back, although if you had, it would have been a sign that I'd waited long enough. I've always been willing to chase after you. I was waiting for you to heal enough that being near me didn't just rip your wounds right open again with every breath I took."

She sat up, clutching the sheet to her, utterly stunned. Being near him had felt *exactly* like that. The rawness of her soul, the ragged ripping at it of his existence, her need to hide, hide, hide from anything that held more feeling, to bury herself as deep as a bear in some cave of snow.

"I should have forced you to go to a therapist somehow. I just—you weren't suicidal, and you weren't homicidal, and I could hardly have you committed, Kai. I *knew* you weren't normal, but I couldn't tell what part was some kind of postpartum depression and what part was the real grief and anger that you had to find a way to work through."

She swallowed with great difficulty, as if she was trying to squeeze some huge marshmallow down her throat whole. "Neither could I," she whispered, hanging her head. "I still can't."

He angled his head against the glass, and she felt him watching her, but she couldn't look at him. She couldn't. *I'm so sorry.*

And then he walked back across the room, sat down on the bed beside her, and put his arm around her, pulling her into his warm chest and pressing a kiss to the top of her head. He didn't say anything. After a moment, she slipped her hands up to his chest and buried her fingertips in her palms so that she wouldn't clench tight fistfuls of his skin. Closing her eyes, she focused on the feel of his arms around her, his body against her face, the scent of him, the warmth. She focused so hard that it made every hair on her body shiver up, and then subside, and then shiver up again.

He brought his other arm to join the first, wrapping around her, but he never said a word. A couple of times he kissed her head again.

"I joined a group here," she said finally, low. "After a while. That first winter, I couldn't be near anybody, I couldn't stand to let anybody in. If your mother hadn't let me have this cabin, I—I don't know what I would have done. Hiked the Appalachian Trail maybe, except I probably would have just curled up and died mid-route." Her mouth twisted in some ghost of her old humor, so strange to feel it this way, about this subject. "It's hard to curl up and die so easily in a warm luxury cabin without the help of hypothermia."

"I wish I could have been there," Kurt said, strained. "Kai—I wish I could have fixed it." His hands flexed against her, his voice deepening grimly. "Instead of making it worse."

She said nothing. What could she say? Every single thing he had tried had made it worse, and yet he had tried so hard. After a moment, she pressed a kiss into his bare chest, for everything words couldn't give him.

"I love you," he said quietly. "Kai."

She began to tremble. Her stomach shook so badly she felt sick from it. She wanted to cover her ears and bury her face to shut out this thing that couldn't possibly be true.

And if it was true, if it was true—oh, God, it made her *sick* how little she deserved it. It made her feel terrified and broken, to try to construct something on the ruins of their old happiness. She could not *do it.* She had *failed.* She was too afraid.

She forced herself away from him, not all the way, but enough distance to make one fact clear to both of them: *I don't deserve this. This can't be.* "You can't possibly."

His lips compressed, such sudden anger blazing up in his eyes that it caught her there, hands still touching his chest, staring back into it. "I'll be the judge of what I'm capable of doing," he said harshly.

She took a shaky breath.

"Fuck," he said wearily and stood again from the bed. Once he had taken a step away from her, though, he just stopped, running his hands through his hair as if he had no idea what to do with them.

"I'm sorry," she said, too low, that marshmallow impossible in her throat. "I guess I can't stop destroying things."

This morning. That beautiful moment when he opened his eyes and smiled at her. Couldn't she have at least stopped herself from destroying that?

"Destroying things?" He half-turned. He really had such a beautiful body, all that elegant, intense strength. "Have you started blaming it all on yourself again? Kai, the doctors said—"

She lifted a hand, pushing that subject away. "Let's not talk about that," she said quietly. "Let's not—I know what the doctors said. Let's let them stay—" She hated so much to say "buried" for those three little hopes of children. "Asleep." In her mind, she envisioned three little mounds covered gently with snow and sighed, but it was a long, quiet, sad sigh. It was one she had made her peace with.

Maybe that long, long frozen year had served some kind of function after all.

Kurt stretched a hand across the distance between them and curved it against her cheek, saying nothing. Tears pricked again. She did not want to ruin his morning completely, but it felt so healing to cry this way, as if the liquid came from snow melting into spring. They were sweeter tears than all the other ones she had cried.

"I meant us," she whispered. "I destroyed us."

His fingers tightened against her cheek. "I'm not destroyed."

Her breath stopped.

"I'm scarred." He withdrew his hand and closed it carefully into a fist at his side. Again it slid in search of a pocket, but found none in which to bury itself. "I'm battered. But I'm still standing, Kai."

Sometimes far too many feelings swirled in a body at once. As if a wind had whipped around a snow statue and brought it to life.

"How about you?" Kurt asked.

She could only stare at him. "Are you giving me *another chance*?" How could he? Despite every indication he kept making that he would like for them to be together again—how could he possibly?

His mouth set, that fine, elegant line of grimness he

had, this man who tried so hard not to fling his anger around blindly. "I wasn't aware I had ever terminated your first chance."

"I thought *I* did. I destroyed my chance."

His mouth went even grimmer, knuckles white by his side. "What the hell did you think our marriage was, a lottery ticket? To be ripped in half when it wasn't the winning number?"

Well, if it was, she had certainly shredded it. "What did *you* think it was?"

He shot her a hard look, revealing an anger in which she could at least believe. Unlike the love, the anger was deserved. "A marriage."

Her breaths came with difficulty, leaving her sick and shaky. "But I *left* you." After first destroying anything and everything about them with every word she could muster.

"Did you really?" He rubbed his fingers over and over against the white terry towel at his thigh. "I always tried to tell myself that you left—you. That you just had to get away from you for a while until, you know—you could come back." He pressed his fingertips into the towel and his thigh until white showed where his knuckles bent back. "I was sorry," he said low, "not to be able to help you with that. I was sorry that everything I tried just made it worse. I was sorry that when you needed it, I couldn't give you the same joy and happiness that you had given me."

"It's not your fault, Kurt. Nobody could have—"

"I wasn't nobody," he interrupted harshly and then stopped himself and shook his head. "I wasn't—well, I guess I was only me."

"Kurt, *don't*—" *Don't say "only".*

He shook his head again, as if he was trying to shake his thoughts into a new direction. "I think I need to go for a walk."

He didn't ask her to come with him, scooping up his clothes and heading toward the door.

"Kurt," she managed, as he reached it. "Don't be humble." *You deserve so much better than me.*

You deserve someone who only gives you laughter and happiness.

And that traitorous, evil thought she had laid to rest so long ago snuck back: *Someone who can have babies like a normal person.* She curled her fingers into the sheets, willing it away.

He paused at the door just long enough to look back at her a steady moment with those gorgeous hazel eyes of his. "Kai. You've always humbled me."

Chapter 9

Humbled him when she gave him all that laughter and life of hers so spontaneously, as if he *deserved* it. Humbled him at their wedding, when she looked up at him with her eyes gone all solemn, but still so, so happy, and said, *I will*. Humbled him when he placed his hand on her belly and thought, awestruck, that she was going to have a *baby*. *His* baby. How did she *do* that? Humbled him when she wept and wept and wept and tried again and all he could do was hold her.

Humbled him when she left him, yes. God, the inadequacy of him to her needs. He'd been worth *nothing*.

That anger pressed up through him again, that sneaky bastard monster with all its snaky heads. He knew she didn't deserve that rage, and he knew he couldn't let it free, but it reared up in him sometimes, all the same.

I'm sorry. He saw her face as she said it, her head bowed, tears filling her eyes, and one of the monster snake-heads laid itself down and just slowly dissipated, like a witch's body touched with water. *I'm so sorry*, she had said another moment, and a second head slunk down to the ground and shriveled into nothing.

He hoped two weren't going to grow back where each one had been. You never knew with anger. Hers had been a wild thing, out of control, there at the end, and nothing could cauterize where those first heads had been and keep them from sprouting back up again, more numerous and stronger than before. He had tried probably way too many things, ending up with far too many heads to fight and all of them focused on him.

Yeah, if ever she got pregnant again—*please, God, let's not try that again—*

oh, but shit, *he would have liked to have a little blonde girl with—*

let it go, let it go.

But if she ever did, they had to have a pact or something. A written contract, that he could take her to a therapist and she would go, and if everything went so wrong again, he would hold that written promise in her face like some magic charm and *will* it to work.

Yeah. Like that marriage contract had worked. That solemn vow of *I will.* She'd broken that one.

And there it was, that goddamn hydra anger. Heads rearing back up, tongues lashing between vicious teeth, ready to strike at his soul.

No, he said, and picked up a handful of snow, pressing it to his forehead. The coolness reminded him of her, of playing in the woods with her, and the anger slumped down, glowering at his mastery of it, as he hiked on.

He passed the most perfect little fir for a Christmas tree, just as tall as he was, a little shaggy on one side, but you could turn that side to the wall. His mother wouldn't have put up with the asymmetry, but Kai wouldn't mind. He stood for a moment, gazing at it, thinking of all the Christmases they had curled up with a tree in the corner of the room. And then thinking of that last Christmas.

That horrible, horrible last Christmas.

He would like to think they could curl up by a fire and a Christmas tree again one day, but was this Christmas too soon for her? Would it hurt more than heal?

He walked on, glancing back at the fir, and eventually came out at the viewpoint to which the path led. From there, the mountains swept down into the valley, everything hushed with snow, a glimpse glowing through the fog of the giant star the little town below hung up on a crane for the holidays.

He brushed snow off the big rock that helped make

this such a perfect lookout point and sat down on it. Gradually, at his stillness, birds began to sneak in around him, and he realized bird seed was scattered on the ground. Three bird feeders had been hung from the trees, made of exquisite, fragile glass. They hadn't been there the last time he had visited the cabin, which meant Kai had hung them, and as soon as he realized that, he knew why there were three.

Emotion tried to strangle him, and he bent to scrub his face with his hands. Oh, Kai.

Kai, sweetheart.

He wished so badly he could have healed her. Made her forget everything. Made it all go away. He had tried, and that had been part of her fury. *I don't want to forget. I'll never forget. You don't understand! You never cared!*

He had cared. Just—she had cared so much more. His care, the care that ripped *him* to pieces, had been focused in a different direction—not on what was growing in her belly, a little knot of cells in which, after the first time, he never again could really believe, but on her. Because her he could believe in. He could see and feel and suffer at what was happening to her.

He sighed heavily and lifted his head to gaze out over the valley again and eye the birds sideways, wondering if she had sighed exactly like that sometimes, right in this spot, if she had lifted her head and taken a deep breath, and just—sighed again. Let it sigh out, sigh on, let some of it sigh away.

Kai, sweetheart.

The birds scattered when he rose and touched each bird feeder, gently and carefully, a tiny stroke of his fingers. He headed back down into the woods and stood a moment under the trees, watching the birds come back, all bright, beautiful colors—goldfinches and cardinals and bluebirds and then the determined brown sparrows.

On the way back down, he stopped in front of that fir tree again for a long time.

Chapter 10

B ook after book on the phases of grief and miscarriages and postpartum depression filled the screen of Kurt's iPad when she turned it on. Kai hesitated, her stomach doing this strange ragged twirl as she stared at them. Her fingers hovered, that close to opening one of the books, and then quickly she shut the reader app, determined to just check the weather, her original intention.

But then she saw the photo folder, and she hesitated again. They had never kept things private like this. Computers, accounts, codes—neither had ever had anything to hide from the other. But now . . .

She opened the folder before she could allow herself to admit that she shouldn't. Just to see what he had been doing, this past year and a half.

But there wasn't anything from the past year and a half.

All the photos were of her. Of them. A scanned copy of the first photo they had ever taken together, with a camera held out in Kurt's hand as they pressed their cheeks together, because he had so wanted to capture them as a couple. She was laughing. His eyes were alight with happiness.

Her on a carousel horse at an amusement park she had talked him into going to—fifth date, still teaching him how to have fun—and she was laughing again. A photo one of their friends had caught of them at a cookout, Kai curled up against his shoulder, Kurt's head angled to look down at her, such a beautiful expression on his face that she wondered why she didn't have that photo tattooed on her heart.

Photos from their wedding, photos from their honeymoon, photos of their camping trip in Banff, photos at friends' houses, a photo at one of his Frisbee tournaments when his team had won and he had lifted her up in his sweaty arms in triumph, as if she was his trophy.

The door opened and she lifted her head quickly, so awash in memories that all the hairs on her body were standing on end from them. "I was—I was just trying to see if we were expecting more snow," she said guiltily.

"And are we?" Kurt asked, scraping his boots in the entrance, not seeming in the least troubled about questions of whether or not she still had the right to look at his iPad without asking. *I wasn't aware that I had terminated your first chance.* In one hand, he carried a saw, one of the hand-crafted artisan tools with gorgeous wooden handles that his mother had featured in a magazine spread, during that period when Anne Winters frequently used this cabin and the different themes she could associate with it for her magazine and on her show. "I saw a—" Kurt hesitated. "Would you come cut down a Christmas tree with me, Kai?"

Her breath caught. She envisioned it so suddenly: them and a Christmas tree and just being *happy.* Maybe not entirely like they used to be, having passed through sadness, but still *happy again.*

"I would like one," he said cautiously, affirming himself like a man who feared he might be putting his foot down on eggshells. Or glass shards.

"I don't know," she said. But she took a deep breath and thought, *I do. I do want one. I do want to be happy.*

Oh, God, I don't deserve him.

She closed his iPad cover carefully over all those photos of them and came to him, standing so close she could feel the cold off his jacket. "Yes, I would." Water from the snow dust melting off his shoulder curled slowly down his sleeve. She touched it, tracing it back up to the melting remains of snow, that she covered with her hand. "I do," she said solemnly, feeling oddly like she had the day she had looked up at him in a church and married him. "I do want one." She took a breath and sighed. "But I can't promise it won't make me cry," she added wistfully. Once upon a time, she almost never really cried, except at sad movies and from joy. She'd cried when he asked her to marry him. She'd been so happy.

He tucked her hair behind her ear and squeezed her shoulder, without comment. Just—compassion. It made her feel so strange—as if he, too, had come to a place of peace over the past year, a place where he didn't try to fix her back into the person he had loved anymore, he just . . . loved her.

But how could that be? She wasn't very lovable now, was she? Wasn't fun, still cried too much, might ruin any laughing moment by suddenly getting struck with the grief of it. And she couldn't stand to force herself or fake herself, to pretend to laugh when she didn't feel like laughing. It was one of the reasons she had lost most of her friends and couldn't even stand to see her family anymore.

But she did want to get a Christmas tree with him. She did. She did want to try again.

She put on her jacket and her boots.

The fog still clung a little, in wisps, to the snow, and teased through the trees like some winter dance of veils, luring the traveler in. The tramp of their boots on the snow cut through it, and Kurt's bare hand closed warm and strong around hers, burying both their hands in his pocket as he dragged the fresh-cut tree behind him with his other arm. She let the grief at not being able to share this moment *also* with at least one of those three little kids—*damn you, God, couldn't you at least have let me keep one of them?*—just ride there quietly, like one of those tendrils of fog. No point chasing it away, there was more where it came from and she would just find herself pursuing its will-o'-the-wisp farther and farther away from the chance of happiness she *did* have and which was holding her hand right now.

Yes, she had chased her grief well off the beaten path more than once already. She didn't need to follow it now. She could concentrate on his hand. On this chance which he claimed was not her second one. On the two of them. They had been very, very happy once, just the two of them, before they had gotten that dream to make their happiness even bigger.

To spread it around. To pass it on.

Oh, God damn it, there was that grief again.

But she breathed it in, breathed it out, letting it drift around her, its wisps teasing as she focused on the feel of Kurt's hand. That beautiful, strong hand, that she had never thought to feel holding hers again.

"You never even thought about moving on?" she asked, low.

He frowned. "No." And after a few crunchy steps, very, very low indeed: "Did you?"

The tree dragged behind them in a soft shush. She let the sound of it slide over her a long time before she finally spoke. "I thought I had to. I thought I had ruined any other choice."

His hand flexed on hers in his pocket, and six slow, steady steps measured out the pause before he spoke. "Kai, I'm sorry if selling the house made you think that. I just really couldn't stand it anymore. It got so I would do anything, rather than come home."

Her throat tightened as she imagined him again, imagined how much it must have hurt. She had been so focused on her other hurt that it had been a long time before she had also had to deal with the fact that she had lost him, too. "I'm sorry," she whispered.

He let go of the tree and picked her up, sandwiching her between him and the nearest pine, as he kissed her. Just kissed her. Tender and gentle but very thorough, taking his time. "I know you are, sweetheart," he said softly, and kissed each of her eyelids closed, and kissed the tear away. "I know." He kissed her again, longer this time, deeper, hunger rising up through his body, pressing into her. "God." He lifted his mouth. "I could drag us into a cave and just be an animal with you for days, do you know that? Just—feel."

"Me, too." She squeezed herself up against him. A cave sounded beautiful. Nothing but darkness and bodies, their bodies, them.

"Unless you've discovered an actual cave around here that I never did, let's quit hiking so damn far from the house," he said.

But he must know perfectly well that they needed those hikes as much as the time in the cave.

At the house, he made his own cave out of her comforter, pulling it over them in the big bed, so that the only thing that existed was the heat of their bodies. Even when it got too hot, she didn't want to come out from under it, and whenever he shrugged the comforter back to breathe cool air, she hid herself under him, pressing into his chest. And he came back to her, kissing her and kissing her, hands running all over her, a silent, intense love-making out of time, no beginning and no end, just the two of them. Just the two of them. The two of them filling their whole world, all that mattered, all that ever need matter.

"You're the most beautiful thing that ever happened in my life," Kai whispered suddenly, clutching at him as if he might melt out of her arms. His arm tightened under her bottom, driving himself deep, deep. "I don't know what I did to deserve you."

She'd thought giving him happiness and a family was what she was doing to deserve him. Once upon a time. And even then, he had always seemed so special to her, with that care and strength and intelligence and that way he had of looking at her across a room. She had always known that she couldn't ever entirely deserve him, that partly she was just lucky. That partly she was just the playful girl who had been smart enough to take him on a hike.

Kurt kissed her deeply, shutting off all words, and

she let them go, let all the thoughts in her go, let herself become just an animal, an animal. Let herself wallow in it mindlessly, wallow in making him an animal, too. Neither spoke again. Maybe you couldn't speak your human language to another and do some of the things they did.

Kurt left her dozing eventually, still under the comforter, still out of time.

She didn't know how long she stayed in the comforter-cave, in no hurry to wake or think or come out. But when she eventually did, she found the tree standing in the corner of the great living room, a careful distance from the fire, and Kurt was at the granite island with half the supplies from his mother's old craft room spread around him, making Christmas ornaments.

Incredible Christmas ornaments, too, the kind that appeared in his mother's magazine and that no average person could get to look like Anne Winters's. Not that Kurt had ever been average, no matter what he thought about himself. "I take it that it's genetic?" Kai said, both amused and impressed. While she rarely applied her own ability for precision to crafts, preferring the work with food, she understood exactly what went into that level of perfect craftsmanship.

Kurt looked around and smiled at her, a small, warm smile. He was halfway through something elaborate with ribbons and glitter, and his hands were occupied. "No, but who do you think she kept testing those kid crafts of hers on when I was little? We both had a hard time of it when I was five and could never get any of her visions for kid crafts to actually work out beautifully, like I was supposed to. But by the time I was eight, I was the model crafting child."

"You have hidden talents." Kai came forward. Glitter streaked across one of his cheeks, little sparkles of white that caught the light every time he shifted his head. "I guess it makes sense, but I've never seen you do anything like this before."

"I started rebelling against it all when I was about ten." That would have also been the age when his father divorced his mother, unable to put up with her ever-increasing need for control, and moved to California. "And moved into sports and, you know, boy things—the kind of thing that drove her crazy. By the time you met me, we'd more or less found an even keel between us, but that didn't mean I had to do crafts for her." That glimmer of his wry smile that she loved so much, the way it was so restrained and yet all that brilliance and subtle humor of his showed through. "Just all her legal contracts."

He finished tying the ribbon and set the ornament on a pan with a dozen others already made: snowflakes, some two-dimensional, some three-dimensional, their heavy card stock thickly covered in fine white and silver glitter. In his hands, per his mother's training, the snowflakes became a very sophisticated, adult craft.

"You can pick the next ornaments," he said. "Are we doing a two-color theme or a hodge-podge?"

They were going to do crafts together? That was so—sweet. So optimistic, so happy. She took a deep breath, trying to make sure she had enough room to let that sweetness come all the way into her soul. She couldn't refuse him in this, not Kurt. Even to protect herself she couldn't. "Have you ever done cinnamon dough ornaments? They're my favorite. They scent the whole house. You can leave them this rustic brown with pretty ribbons, or your mom did an issue where she covered them with glitter. If we did that, we could do birds pecking through the snow, cardinals, bluebirds."

He looked up at her suddenly. Their eyes held. "Kai, don't do something sad," he said softly.

She hadn't thought about it, and now she did, her little bird feeders and . . . "Oh." She took another deep breath as her heart tightened, and then she sighed it out. "Well, growly brown bears in the woods, and stars, and stockings, and holly. And—and maybe some birds. I can have some birds if I want them."

He took her hands in his gluey, glittery fingers and pulled her between his thighs to kiss her. "I think I got glue in your hair," he said, when they surfaced. "And you glitter now."

She smiled at him, wondering if this was her Christmas miracle—that he still seemed so determined to love her. No matter what.

Oh, but how could he? It couldn't be as fresh and bright and happy as it had once been, could it? It never could be again.

She pressed her head down on his shoulder just a moment, drawing strength or belief, and then went to get the cinnamon and allspice.

It was so easy to start laughing, making Christmas crafts together. It was so easy to have fun. Kurt was insanely good at making them, for one thing, and he made her laugh more and more and tease him as he came up with one thing out of his childhood after another. Why had they never done this before? Well, she supposed because Christmas crafts were the kind of thing a mom typically pulled out to work on with her kids, for one—the grief squeezed and sighed and let her be—and probably Kurt had more than had his fill of Christmas crafts as his mother's only child. As a couple, they had kept with her own tradition of collecting ornaments wherever they traveled and filling the tree with those. She had saved the crafting sessions for what she thought would be their later, that time in their lives when kids would fill their house.

That time that had just not been meant to be.

So now they went all out. They even tried the white feather Christmas trees from his mother's latest December issue, and when Kai looked up and discovered Kurt concentrating fully on his craft, oblivious to the feather glued to his cheek, a giggle burst out of her, and she clapped her hands over her belly in surprise, not quite sure where it had come from. Once that first giggle had bubbled itself out of her, more came suddenly, like a pot that had finally been brought to boil, and she giggled and giggled, until she felt as effervescent as a glass of champagne. Kurt upended the bag of white feathers over her head in punishment for laughing at him, and then pulled her to him again, kissing her and kissing her, as the feathers drifted off her hair, gliding softly over her cheeks and tickling his hands.

The scent of cinnamon and cloves filled the house. She made cookies again, while the cinnamon dough was baking in one oven and the glue on the snowflakes was drying, and that added scents of butter and sugar and everything homey. Then she realized it was past lunchtime, and she heated up last night's soup and then, while she was thinking of it, started a stew in the Dutch oven for that night. Through this flurry of cooking, Kurt chopped onions, carrots, and whatever he was told, looking very happy.

I can still make him happy?

I can, can't I? I can still make him happy.

That was kind of a precious miracle in and of itself.

She kissed him, and he set the knife carefully far away from them as he kissed her back—which was so like him, that care and attention. She kissed him more for it, and then, and then—all the pain she had caused him rose up in her, and she pulled back, ashamed, knowing she didn't deserve this. *Damn it, would the weight of her guilt never go away?*

Kurt must have thought her withdrawal was from another wave of grief for the miscarriages, because he squeezed her shoulder and pulled a feather out of her hair, going back to work on the potatoes without comment. By the time the ornaments were dry enough to let them decorate the tree, a plethora of scents filled the house to bursting: cinnamon, cookies, stew, the fir itself as it prickled over her arms, the fire Kurt started. Given that she was a food stylist who often did her work here, scents of food had filled this house ever since she had moved into it. And yet it was so different when the scents were shared.

So much warmer, so much more full. As if life was full. Not this great empty thing she had to get through.

She kissed him again, and he pulled her into his arms, squeezing her far too hard.

He couldn't seem to let go. Even when she had to wiggle for freedom because her lungs started protesting, he couldn't loosen his arms, and when she squeaked, he took them down onto the plush rug in front of the fire. The early winter evening was lowering by then, gray deepening toward night over the snow, and their fire and their tree lights glowed over their faces in the otherwise unlit room.

Kurt captured her wrists over her head as the only thing he seemed to know to do with his hands to keep them from squeezing her too tightly. When she tried to pull free, his hold tightened. "Kurt," she protested, half-laughingly.

"In a minute." The firelight gilded over his cheekbones, throwing them into relief, his face intense, severe.

Arousal washed through her. Of course it did. How could she help it? They had discovered a long, long time ago that sometimes she liked that game. And oh, so did he. But she said, "Kurt, no. I want my hands free."

With some difficulty, he pulled his hands from her wrists and sank them instead into the thick rug, digging into it.

"I want to do this," she said softly, wrapping her arms around him and squeezing him as tightly as he had her.

He let his body lower onto hers with the heavy voluptuousness of a man sinking into a bed after a long, brutal day. The warmth of him rushed from her fingertips to her toes. She ran those fingertips over him, seeking still more of that warmth, like an impossible addiction.

"I want to do this," she whispered, unbuttoning his shirt and finding her way in to his skin. She shivered with the pleasure of it, as if she hadn't just felt his skin that morning, as if it had been years.

The white Christmas lights sparkled over his strong, smooth back when she bared it. She chased them over his skin, fascinated, stroking them as if they were a dream she could capture. On the tree, the lights shimmered off the glitter of the snowflakes and brown bears and red cardinals, sparkling over this dream, this dream she could have.

Still.

He would still let her have him.

That was such an incredible thing.

He made love to her intensely, in the firelight and the tree lights, kissing her everywhere, being kissed everywhere, stroking her too deeply, gripping her too hard, and breathing in hard gasps of pleasure when she gripped and stroked him, too. He rolled her over him and sat her up astride him for what seemed to be the pure pleasure of seeing her there, of stroking the lights over *her* skin, maybe of believing in her. He rolled her under him again in a sudden, hard rush, as if he had to capture her beneath him before she disappeared.

"I love you," she said suddenly, and he jerked, his hands spasming on her body.

"I love you so much," she said, and he kissed her urgently, whether to shut the words up or to drink them straight from her mouth, she couldn't tell.

She kissed him back, giving him the words through her kiss, through her touch. *I love you so much. How could you love me?*

I got so bogged down in what I lost, but I never lost you?

"I love you so much," she whispered again to his shoulder, that strong, strong shoulder, the gorgeous bone and sinew and muscle of it.

He slipped his hand between her face and his body and covered her mouth, forcing her head down to the floor until she was pinned there by his hand silencing her. She stared at him over it. His face could have cut the air with its severity, his eyes glowing in the firelight, almost beseeching, as if she was torturing him.

But I do, she tried to say, the protest muffled against his hand.

But I really do.

His palm hardened, his other hand dragging fiercely down from her breast, over her belly, to take her sex, spearing her in one aggressive thrust of his finger.

She yelped a little, and that, too, got crushed by his hand on her mouth. She tried to twist her head back and forth, to shake him off her, but he held her, and her body yielded to his mastery in one helpless rush of arousal. Making itself ready for whatever he wanted.

Oh, God, she had always loved this game. And yet it was different now.

It wasn't a game.

His eyes glittered, his touch so ferocious, so much anger in him suddenly, this wild beast of anger that bucked against even his control.

I do love you, she told him with her hands, shaping those beautiful cheekbones of his, that mouth that hardened so much when her fingers stroked over it. *I do.* She petted the words over his hair, which had gotten just a little too long, as if he just could not bring himself to care about getting it cut.

Shut up, his finger said, spearing her deep, holding her impaled. When she wriggled against it, the heel of his palm firmed on her pubic bone, holding her down, and all her body's effort to adjust had to go into the squeeze of her inner muscles around his finger, into the heady release of all tension, the softening.

She dragged her hands over those gorgeous arm muscles of his, all lean and hardened now. *You don't understand. I really, really do.*

I'll make you shut up, his thumb said against her

clitoris. *I'll make you.* She shivered with the pleasure and the invasion, aroused more and more every time she tried to twist and failed to twist free. The arousal pressed at her, almost brutally fast, the edge coming up so quickly . . .

Please, Kurt. She tried to beg for more, for release, and she couldn't. Only with her eyes, and yet when she tried to catch his eyes, tried to beg him, his own eyes glittered, ungentle, dangerous. *Please just—do it,* she tried to plead with a buck of her hips.

But he wouldn't let her hips buck. He eased his thumb up from her clitoris and twisted his finger in her, slow and deep and relentless, at every attempt.

She began to pant, wanting to kiss him so desperately, wanting to fling herself at him and wrap herself around him and drag him into her. But his hand pressed down on her lips unyieldingly, and the line of his mouth was bitter-hard.

Please, please, please. She dragged her hands down his arm, pressing his thumb back against her.

The edge of his teeth showed at that, something cruel and fierce, and he took his thumb and drove her toward her peak while he watched her, that torturer's merciless regard, as if her orgasm was her confession or her punishment.

Kurt, Kurt, Kurt, she tried to cry out his name as the waves hit her, to be saved by him, to be held by him, to find her solace in the wild, rocking pleasure of it. But she couldn't do that either. She could only come, clutching to his wrist as he made her do so, lost and unable to speak.

He made her come and come and come, as if he wanted to *torture* her with her own pleasure, and she couldn't speak to stop him, he wouldn't let her.

Then he took her, in long, deep relentless thrusts, his hands at last slipping to either side of her head to brace himself while she came apart again at the pleasure of being so used. *Oh, God, use me. Please use*

me. "I love you, I love you, I love you," she scrambled
out as the waves of pleasure mounted again, driving
her madder and madder with each slow thrust.

He kissed her this time to shut her up, thrusting
his tongue into her as if in his head he was thrusting
something else, and brought his thumb back into play,
driving her mercilessly with each thrust of his body and
the deep, relentless, silencing kisses, until she was
caught everywhere in him, unable to think or speak or
do anything but yield, shattering for him over and over,
until his fingers dug cruelly into her butt with his last
thrust as he came, too.

It was a long time before he rolled away. He lay still
on the rug for a while, and eventually rolled back on his
side to look at her. His hand came up to stroke gently
over her mouth, and then he leaned closer to kiss all
around the edges of her lips, which still felt crushed.

"I'm sorry," he said low. "The last time I thought
you loved me, you left me in the morning. I didn't mean
to let it out in quite that way."

She nodded. *I'm sorry.* "I did love you. Too much.
And I just couldn't—I couldn't—" Her voice broke, and
he took her hand, holding it securely. "I couldn't love
anymore. I just couldn't. Not then. You know?"

She had tried to tell him this the day before, and
yet no matter how many times she said it, it seemed so
stupid, so worthless, to say she *couldn't*. Couldn't love
him, of all people. *Can't never could,* her dad would
always say cheerfully when she was a kid balking at
some challenge. You always *could*, if you tried hard
enough. Some days it had felt as if she was trying with
everything in her. And failing. She had hated those
days. She had not wanted to try. She had just wanted
to curl up in the snow and die.

"No," Kurt said. "I don't know. But I read about it. I
can try to understand."

"You—you've never reached the point where you
couldn't love me?" How could that possibly be? The
screaming, weeping woman she had turned into, out of

all that life and fun and laughter he had married?

"No, Kai. I never have."

"It just hurt so much, to love," she whispered. "It was like my heart had been shattered into all these shards of glass and it pierced me every single time it tried to beat. I had to hide."

He said nothing, lying on his side in the firelight and Christmas lights, stroking her knuckles as he watched her.

"And I was hurting you. I couldn't keep hurting you that way. I had to get away."

"Kai. I could take it, you screaming. It was the least I could do." He shifted back to her until the length of their bodies touched, covering her belly with his hand. "Because I couldn't do this. I could only watch as it— broke you." The lights shimmered across the sudden sheen his eyes. "Shit." His hand left her belly to dash across his eyes suddenly, and then he rolled away to lie on his back, lashes pressed firmly down on his cheeks, as he breathed long careful breaths.

She curled into him, wrapping one arm around him and pressing her cheek into his shoulder. They lay there for a while, in the heat of the fire.

"You remember all those *stupid* things I used to do, to try to keep it from breaking you?" Kurt asked softly.

She nodded against his shoulder. *Just don't think about it, Kai. Wait until we know for sure.* Or, after, *Let's go on a trip, sweetheart. What do you say to the Bahamas?* No matter how much she loved him, she had still hated him for those ideas. "I know you meant well," she murmured. "I know you wanted to help."

"I suspect you have no idea how much I wanted to help. The same way there are things you felt that I can't ever really know, I think I have some feelings that you won't ever be able to understand completely, either."

She kissed his shoulder and then just lay there against him, stroking his chest. Sometimes maybe that was all there was left to do, accept that two people could love each other and yet their minds and hearts not always work the same. They fell asleep that way, waking to full darkness and the scent of dinner.

There was something peculiarly and profoundly lovely about sitting in the firelight with bowls of stew before them, eating together. "Is it Christmas Eve?" she asked suddenly.

He nodded.

Her mouth twisted. "I was—trying not to keep track, this year." In her vision of the way her life should have gone, that third baby was supposed to have been born at midnight, her little miracle baby, and a great star would shine in the heavens and all the world would be made right.

He reached across and touched her hand.

"I'm glad you're here," she said suddenly. And, with a quiet wonder: "It's a—it's a *good* Christmas."

"Oh, God, it's so much better than last year," he said, heartfelt, taking both her hands. His eyes searched her face, and his voice went very low and careful: "Kai, I know how happy you made me. But have you ever thought that maybe it's taking you so long to recover because—I might have helped make you happy, too?"

"Kurt." She could only stare at him. It hurt her so deeply that she might have left him thinking so little of himself. "Of *course* that's part of why it's taking me so long to be happy again. Because I destroyed *us, too*, the one thing that could have kept on being as beautiful as it was from the very first moment it was conceived. You were why I was so happy. You didn't know that?"

He shook his head, slowly but very firmly. "I know you said that sometimes, Kai, but you were always happy. Before, I mean. The first moment I met you, you were happy."

"You were there, weren't you?" she pointed out simply.

His gaze was incredulous. "Kai. There is *no way*

you looked across that garden and lit up that way because of *me*. That's not—I don't hit people that way. I've met your family. You're just happy people. You like to laugh and play and—I got lucky. Well, I put a lot of effort into making sure I was the man who got that lucky, but you know what I mean."

He had gotten lucky. To find her. Wasn't that the craziest thing for him to think? "I don't think you know what *I* mean. Yes, I was always a laughing, fun-loving person. Compared to yours, my family looks like a non-stop swing dance, I guess." She had spoken to her family less and less with each miscarriage and barely at all in the past year. They hadn't known what to do with that much grief, and she hadn't known what to do with their need for her to get over it again and just laugh with them. And get back with Kurt and be the sweetheart couple in which they had so delighted before. "But you were the reason I was . . . *happy*." She pressed her fist to her heart, trying to show something deeper. "And yes, you did hit me that way. You made my whole body kick awake the first moment I looked up and saw you watching me, and I *liked* it. And then, when you were courting me—"

He winced a little in embarrassment at the word *courtship*, the way he always did, and a little grin came up out of somewhere inside her, surprising her again by how readily it wanted to spark out, just like her laughter used to. Some moments, he made her feel as if she might one day become a fully happy person once again, given enough time. Given him.

"You were so *hot*," she said and had to rub her hands over her face as it surged through her, the memory of how helplessly attracted she had felt, the way every cell in her body seemed to pull toward him like filings to a super magnet, and how she had loved every minute of it. Never an instant's fear, never even a second of trepidation at the possible consequences of giving him all her heart. He had always seemed like such a sure, strong, perfect person to receive all her life.

That old fearless heart was changed now, had learned fear, and yet—here he was. Still there for her. Still taking care. "Really hot," she whispered.

His own grin showed, a surprised kick of pleasure. She used to be able to make him blush by telling him how hot he was, streaking color across those beautiful cheekbones, his whole face growing severe in the struggle to get the blush to die down. She had *adored* it.

"You still are, you know," she told him, and—it was so hard to tell with the firelight, but was that the blush? He wasn't trying to fight it, if so, because his face hadn't taken on that adorable blush-fighting sternness, but was instead more vulnerable, more open—hopeful.

His hands pulled on hers, not so hard as to force, but more like a yearning for her. "Kai. Come back to me. Let's work on being happy again. Together. Not alone. I think we're so much more likely to actually reach that happiness again, if we do it together."

"I want to," she whispered. "I really, really want to. If you're sure."

"Kai, sweetheart." Now he did pull her into his lap. His body was sure and strong and held in it, maybe, a thread of anger that tightened it, even as he tried to keep it reassuring. "I've always been sure." *You were the one who wasn't.* But he didn't say it. He'd always been so good at mastering his own anger. Not like her, when that alien anger had taken possession of her after the last miscarriage, had whipped her—and them— around like they were debris caught in its twister. Within only a few seconds, that thread of tension in his body calmed, and he just held her, watching the tree.

And it was, she realized. A good Christmas. He was her miracle. She was beginning to understand now that he always had been.

* * *

94

Hours later, Kurt lay stroking the length of his wife's body, from shoulder to hip, quietly, watching the Christmas tree, too contented to go to sleep and risk waking to find her crying and leaving him again. He knew his distrust might not be fair to her, but he probably wouldn't lose that fear for a long, long time, the same way he hadn't lost the heartbreak of his parents' divorce—and what it meant to him, the essential loss of his father—for years and years, the same way she wouldn't lose the grief over those miscarriages ever, not completely. Life was like that. It dealt you some things that changed you and that you had to deal with, even when you thought they were too cruel, even when you believed that no human should ever have to deal with a blow so cruel. He would have done anything to keep Kai from learning how much life could hurt, but he hadn't had any more ability to stop those losses than she had.

So he stroked her body, profoundly happy to be able to, yet sad, too, because—well, he knew what day their third try was supposed to be born as well as she did. He was glad she was sleeping through midnight. That damn miracle birth hour. He'd had to turn off the radio the day after Halloween last year and listen to nothing but classical music and audio books—usually on dealing with grief—to get him through until January. All those fucking songs about a sweet child cherished by a tender mother, laying his head to rest in a manger and all that. Fuck God, that's what he had thought. *You can get a virgin to give birth to your kid, but you can't let my wife have ours? Fuck You.*

Fuck Santa Claus, too, while he was at it, and all the songs about him. He would have liked to play Santa Claus. See a little kid's eyes light up at all the presents under a tree. *Fuck.*

Those hydra heads rose, and the anger was catching at him, trying to drag him under, when Kai drew a deep breath and started to sing.

Very quietly, her voice so soft. *"Silent night—"*

Oh, fuck, Kai, don't. Don't sing that. Don't rip us to shreds again. Don't do that to yourself. Don't do that to me, God damn it.

"Holy night—"

Oh, shit. He tightened his arm around her waist. But she didn't stop, her voice trembling just a little bit. And so he laid his tenor under hers, giving her voice that support because what else could he do? He couldn't carry the baby. He couldn't drown under a tidal wave of hormones when he lost the baby. He could only support.

"All is calm, all is bright."

He wrapped his arm around her waist, settling his body more closely against her back. His voice nearly gave out on him at the line *mother and child.* But hers didn't, soft and quiet and sure.

"Holy infant, so tender and mild."

And very, very softly at the end, their voices blending: *"Sleep in heavenly peace. Slee-ep in heavenly peace."*

A white light from the Christmas tree sparkled once over her golden hair as her voice faded away, a tiny caress of light that only he saw. When he tried to touch it, it was gone, and yet his fingers tingled from it. She gave a very long, slow sigh and turned her body into his, nestling into him and wrapping her arms around him.

And then she really did sleep. And so did he.

Chapter 11

Morning dawned quietly happy. The happiness stayed cautious, clinging closely to them, afraid to fling itself about too joyously on this delicate day. And yet, it was there—in the air, in the touch of hands, in the way they didn't look each other too long in the eyes, in case they scared it away by staring at it too hard.

Kai made hot chocolate and French toast, and Kurt did the strawberry hearts, proving that the model crafting child could branch out from stock paper and glitter when he wanted to.

Then he gave the strawberries funny faces, and then he set a line of them marching across the whipped cream like little strawberry soldiers to attack her French toast fortress, on the snow-cream top of which her heart was guarded.

She started to laugh, a sound that made his face relax in relief, and kissed him. "Merry Christmas, Kurt."

"Merry Christmas, sweetheart. I love you."

For their Christmas present to each other, they curled up on the couch and looked at all their old photos of happy times, and Kurt talked softly and persuasively of that old trip idea of his. *Could we now, Kai? Could we please? Just the two of us, escape somewhere crazy, for, I don't know, a month, two, pack our lives with something vivid and fun. Hell, we can take a year and do a whole world tour if you want. Ride elephants. Get chased by rhinoceroses. Set a prayer wheel spinning on top of some Tibetan mountain.*

He braced after he said it, doubtless still remembering the way she had screamed at him the last time he suggested this idea. But that level of rage, at least, had faded a long time ago, as her hormones rebalanced.

The hurt hadn't left with the rage, of course. If anything, the rage had been a protective shield against the fullness of that hurt. Even six months ago, it would have been too soon still to bring up this trip idea. Some wounds couldn't be "fixed", no matter how much someone else might want to fix them; sometimes they just needed a lot of time to heal. But now—

She nodded, firmly, and his face lit, and they called up maps and guidebooks and plotted where they would most like to go. It was a little difficult—anticipating *fun* and *life* felt all rusty—but it got better with practice, as if each little touch, each little smile, each photo of a possibility was another drop of oil.

When his mother called and asked Kurt if he was coming to Christmas dinner, and he asked Kai, she said yes a little warily, because it was her first step back into the world. Still, the thought of his mother's cool control was a relief compared to her own family's chaos of wrapping paper and playing nieces and nephews. She could start back into the world with baby steps. "Although I never could figure out what your mother meant by letting me have this cabin. It's almost as if she *wanted* us to be separated."

Kurt was silent for a moment as he helped them off the couch. "I always thought it was proof that my mother actually has a heart."

Kai whipped her head up to stare at him. People close to Anne rarely suspected her of having a heart, Kurt least of all. And she didn't see how the cabin proved the contrary.

"I was seven and nine when she had her own miscarriages," Kurt said very quietly. Shock ran through Kai, a strange woman-to-woman current of pain, of understanding. *Oh. Oh, you know, too.* It was as if there should be some little sign, a woman's hand touching her belly maybe, this secret code of a sorority of sorrow. "I didn't really understand back then what happened to her, why that cold crept in on her and she got even more controlling, so difficult my father just left her."

Oh, Anne. Kai saw the frost-blond bob, the strong jaw and ever-controlled profile, felt against her cheek the little air-kisses of the woman who never let herself get too close. Whose media presence and role of perfectionism was its own force field around her, creating a bubble where she could get everything right.

"I just knew I couldn't reach her myself," Kurt said low. "And never have been able to reach her again. Not so I could tell."

Oh, Kurt. Kurt, Kurt, Kurt. The sudden, incredible realization that he had braved the greatest pain from his childhood, for her: that of having his world fall to pieces, of being shut out. He must have been as helpless against that destruction then as he had been when his life was destroyed a second time as an adult, and yet, for her—he had still tried his hardest to fight it. He had still faced it.

"I think she gave you what she needed for herself back then and never had, because there were too many things she couldn't step away from. But of course, given that it's my mother, it's hard to tell." His mouth twisted wryly. "She did agree to give me an excuse to come up here, though, when I asked her. And she was the one who made the decision to leave us here alone— without warning me, I should mention. I had planned to have people here for more padding. More"—he flexed his fingers, almost as if he was testing the fit of a glove—"armor." He shook his head and closed that hand firmly around hers, warm and sure. "Stupid armor," he murmured so softly she didn't think she was meant to hear. "As if you ever got to wear any."

She hesitated and gestured around to the snow-covered mountains, the isolated cabin.

"Ah." He nodded. "Maybe if you can't have armor, you do need a lot of distance from the world. When you're—wounded." The oddest look crossed his face. "My mother—the person who understood."

"My family never could," she said. "They were too—

happy."

"Yes, I thought of that, how happy your family always was. I had had to learn how to deal with my parents' divorce. And, you know, my mother. She takes a certain amount of strength. But you never had any practice at all, did you?"

No. Happy childhood, happy family, easy time in school, happy marriage to the most wonderful man . . . it had been so easy to have a beautiful life, up until then. She had thought working in top kitchens was the most brutal thing possible in life, and she had shifted away from that brutality into the calmer intensity of food styling, easily enough. She had had no idea. How could *she* not have the babies she wanted? She was— she was *happy*. Unhappy things were for—unhappy people.

What an idiot she had been.

A happy idiot, though.

Images flashed across her mind of all the women in her support group, of her own mother-in-law, the cool, distant Anne. One of the leaders of her support group often said that they weren't supposed to think about *deserving* and *not deserving*, that it was a cruel concept made to hurt. But Kai struggled with it, as with everything else.

In her bedroom—their bedroom now?—she touched her jewelry box, stroking it a moment, eyeing him sideways as he buttoned a pressed, white shirt. She had always found it so hot when he dressed for dinner with his mother. It had *always* made her palms itch with the desire to unbutton him again, to wrinkle his shirt, to tousle his hair, to make him late, but to make him late laughing, every cell of his body sated and relaxed.

His wedding ring glinted from time to time as his fingers moved on the buttons.

She swallowed and looked back at the jewelry box. And then, on a breath, she opened it and reached into the little secret compartment in the back. Beside her, Kurt's hands went still on his buttons.

Taking the rings out, she bit her lip, looking up at him. And then she held them out to him tentatively, afraid to ask, despite everything he had said and done, still afraid to hope that much for forgiveness.

But he fisted his hands and thrust them into his pockets. "I didn't take them off in the first place," he said low and harshly. "If you want them back on your finger, Kai, you put them the fuck back on. You make the choice."

She stared at him, and then her eyes filled with tears because he was so right about that. She started to slide them onto her fingers, wedding band first.

His hand closed suddenly over both of hers, stopping the act. "But if you put them on—they stay on," he said roughly. "You promise me—you *promise me*—that if ever anything like this happens again, you'll let me take you to counseling. We can put it in writing, if you want, so I can hold the damn contract up in your face when you balk and make you stick to it."

Kai laughed despairingly. "You can't—I can't put you through this *again*. If this happens again, you have to find someone else."

He stared at her and then suddenly grabbed her chin, too hard, to force her to look at him. "Kai, *no, I don't*. We don't *know* what might happen. You *might* decide one day that you want to try one more time, and we don't know how that might work out or how much it might hurt if it doesn't. We might adopt, and something happen. One of us might get cancer. Someone might get in a car accident and have brain damage or lose a limb. *We don't know anything.* We're not the same people who couldn't imagine much worse in our lives than maybe breaking a toe playing Frisbee. But that doesn't mean I don't love you, *God.*" He flung his hand away from her chin. "That's what I promised to love you through."

She bent her head, her eyes stinging, so humbled

by him. "I love you, too," she whispered. "I just—I just couldn't drag myself out of it."

"I know. Kai, I've read every book there is to read on the subject. I may never feel it the same way you feel it—it hurt you so much worse than it hurt me—but I *understand*. I would have done anything I could to make it better. That's why I let you go, in the end, because it was the only thing left to do. The only thing you thought would work."

"I'm so sorry," she whispered, as if she could never say it enough.

"So am I, Kai. I'm sorry that I couldn't help. I'm sorry that I couldn't bear it for you. I'm sorry that all I did was make it hurt you so much worse, until you had to get away from me. My God, I'm sorry. Do you know how fucking *small* it is, to be a man, and watch my wife be destroyed for *my* sake, as she tries to have *my* kid, and not be able to do one damn thing about it? I'm sorry. And I'm angry. And like you, I just have to get through that. To the other side. But Kai—" He stretched across the distance between them and closed both hands strongly around hers. "There's no point in getting to the other side, if it's not with you."

She took a deep breath, sucking in all his strength, all his persistence. "I know. That's one of the things that was so hard, after I started getting over the depression. Knowing I didn't deserve you any more." Oh, damn, there was that word again, that her support group tried to stop themselves from using. "That I'd lost you."

He stared at her. "You don't—*deserve*—fuck, Kai. Are you *kidding* me? *You didn't come back to me because you didn't think I'd take you*? God, Kai. I would have crawled on my hands and knees. You were so damned brave. You tried so damned hard. I was *worthless*. I don't even know what you think the word *deserve* means."

Her throat knotted. "You've never been worthless, Kurt. Never. Never. I'm so sorry I—"

He placed his hand over her mouth. Gently this time. "I think you've said that enough, sweetheart. All I needed to know was that you were sorry you left me and ready to try again. Now let that go, Kai. You suffered enough, without spending the rest of your life beating yourself up for how hard the suffering was for you to handle on top of it." His gaze ran from her face to her belly, and he hesitated, but then he curled his hand gently over her abdomen, pulling her in for a careful hug with his hand protecting her womb. "Forgive yourself," he whispered to her hair. "Kai, sweetheart, not one single thing that happened was your fault. Not one—single—thing. Remember that, honey."

Her mouth twisted, bittersweet and weary, but with that whisper of hope. "You sound like my support group."

"Good, then, I've gotten one thing right."

She buried her face against his chest. "Forgiveness hurts," she admitted very low.

His hand rubbed her hair heavily. "It all hurts, honey. I would take it from you, if I could. But all I can do—all I've ever been able to do—is my best to share it."

I love you so much, she thought into his chest. But the hurt of the words this time was a sweeter, gentler ache, as if a mass of toxins that had gotten caught in the idea of *love* had been squeezed out and rinsed clean. She stepped back enough to look into his face and touch his cheek. "Kurt. Don't beat yourself up either. You did everything you could. I just wish—I hadn't hurt you so much. I still don't understand how you can be willing to try again, when you know how unhappy it can be."

He shook his head. "Kai. What did you think it meant, when I said I loved you? That love was just this bright, happy thing?"

She hesitated and shrugged a little, opening her hands. Kind of, yes. *Wasn't* that what it was? Brightness and happiness? Or at least what it was supposed to be?

His hand curved around her face. "So did I, maybe," he said quietly. "But when it wasn't so bright or happy—that didn't mean I wanted to let it go."

Her eyes filled.

"Or let you go," he said very softly.

The tears spilled over.

"Kai."

"I just still don't understand," she whispered. "How you can love me even now. There's a whole huge part of me that doesn't believe you can ever love me, ever again. Not really. How could you?"

His thumb traced one of her tears away. "Because you didn't know I could still love you, when you weren't laughing, when you were ugly and desperate, when your life was hard?"

She shook her head, crying openly now. No, she hadn't known that. She still didn't understand it.

"Well." He bent and kissed her, tasting the tears off her lips. "Now you do."

End

THANK YOU

Thank you so much for reading! This was one of those stories that I just had to write, and I hope it spoke to you as powerfully as it did me. Reviews, of course, are always welcome.

If you're intrigued by stories about a marriage in trouble, I also deal with this theme (albeit much less grief-ridden) in another novella *Turning Up the Heat,* which is also a prequel to my latest series, La Vie en Roses, a series set in the world of flower and fragrance production in Provence.

If you're looking for something lighter, check out the Amour et Chocolat series, a series about among top Parisian chocolatiers and pâtissiers and the women they live to impress. The first in the series is *The Chocolate Thief,* but each book stands alone. Make sure to sign up for my newsletter if you want to know when the next book in this series comes out.

Meanwhile, you can always find me and other readers on Facebook or my website for regular temptations of fantastic chocolate and other kinds of fun.

For a glimpse of *The Chocolate Rose* and a complete list of current books, keep reading.

AN EXCERPT FROM THE CHOCOLATE ROSE

The
Chocolate
Rose

LAURA FLORAND

Jo knew the third time she missed the damn town that she was going to get there too late. Sainte-Mère. How many Sainte-Mères existed off the Côte d'Azur, and how many roads to those towns were under construction?

She should never have accepted a stick shift from the car rental place. If they had held an automatic for her *per her reservation*, she would at least be negotiating these cobblestoned streets, narrower than her car, without fearing she would shift gears wrong and end up in a wall. "I don't think I'm going to be able to get back before tomorrow morning, at this rate," she told her oldest sister on the phone. "I'll have to catch a late train. Cover for me."

"How?" Estelle asked.

"I don't know!" Jo cried, frantically trying to back down a near-vertical slope the size of a piece of spaghetti, in order to allow a car to pass coming the other way. "I'm sick or something and don't want to expose him. You can come up with something!"

It was twelve-thirty when she finally fit her car down the small spiral ramp that passed for the entrance to the parking lot for the old walled part of town. Plane trees shaded the little parking area, and she climbed a staircase from it to the *place* below Gabriel Delange's restaurant.

The scent of jasmine wafted over her as she stepped into the *place*, delicate and elusive, as the breeze stirred vines massed over sun-pale walls. A surprisingly quixotic and modern fountain rippled water softly in the center of a tranquil, shaded area of cobblestones. She stopped beneath the fountain's stylized, edgy angel, dipping her hand into the water streaming from the golden rose it held. *Fontaine Delange*, said a little plaque.

He had a city fountain named after him already? Well, why not? There were only twenty-six three-star restaurants in France, eighty in the world. He had put this little town on the map.

His restaurant, Aux Anges, climbed up above the *place* in jumbled levels of ancient stone, a restored olive mill. She would have loved to sit under one of those little white parasols on its packed terrace high above, soaking up the view and exquisite food, biding her time until the kitchens calmed down after lunch. But, of course, his tables would be booked months in advance. In another restaurant, she might have been able to trade on her father's name and her own nascent credentials as a food writer, but the name Manon was not going to do her any favors here.

The scents, the heat, the sound of the fountain, the ancient worn stone all around her, all seemed to reach straight inside her and flick her tight-wound soul, loosing it in a rush. *Stop. It will be all right. Your father is out of immediate danger, has two other daughters, and will survive a day without you. Take your time, take a breath of that hot-sweet-crisp air.* Relief filled her at the same time as the air in her lungs. That breath smelled nothing like hospitals, or therapists' offices, or the stubborn, heavy despair in her father's apartment that seemed as unshakeable as the grime in the Paris air.

She walked past an art gallery and another restaurant that delighted in welcoming all the naive tourists who had tried showing up at Aux Anges without reservations. A little *auberge*, or inn, gave onto the *place,* jasmine vines crawling all over its stone walls, red geraniums brightening its balconies.

She turned down another street, then another, weaving her way to a secret, narrow alley, shaded by buildings that leaned close enough for a kiss, laundry stretching between balconies. Jasmine grew everywhere, tiny white flowers brushing their rich scent across her face.

Kitchen noises would always evoke summer for her, summer and her visits to France and her father. The open windows and back door of Aux Anges let out heat, and the noises of knives and pots and people yelling, and a cacophony of scents: olive oil, lavender, nuts, meat, caramel . . .

As she approached the open door, the yelling grew louder, the same words overheard a million times in her father's kitchens: *"Service! J'ai dit service, merde,* it's going to be ruined. *SERVICE, S'IL VOUS PLAÎT!"*

"—Fast as we can, *merde – putain,* watch out!"

A cascade of dishes. Outraged yells. Insults echoed against the stone.

She peeked through the door, unable to resist. As a child and teenager, she had been the kid outside a candy shop, confined to her father's office, gazing at all that action, all that life: the insane speed and control and volcanic explosions as great culinary wonders were birthed and sent forth to be eaten.

At least fifteen people in white and black blurred through a futuristic forest of steel and marble. Four people seemed to be doing the yelling, two chefs in white, two waiters in black tuxedos, separated by a wide counter and second higher shelf of steel: the pass, through which elegant plates slipped into the hands of waiters, who carried them into the dining rooms with— ideally—barely a second's pause between when the plate was finished and when it headed toward the customer who was its destination. A wave of profound nostalgia swept Jolie.

"Connard!" somebody yelled.

"C'est toi, le connard, putain!"

A big body straightened from the counter closest to the door and turned toward the scene, blocking her view of anything but those broad shoulders. Thick, overlong hair in a rich, dark brown, threaded with gold like a molten dark caramel, fell over the collar of the big man's chef's jacket, a collar marked with the *bleu, blanc, rouge* of a Meilleur Ouvrier de France. That *bleu, blanc, rouge* meant the chef could only be one person, but he certainly wasn't skinny anymore. He had filled into that space she had used to only imagine him taking up, all muscled now and absolutely sure.

His growl started low and built, built, until it filled the kitchen and spilled out into the street as a full-bodied beast's roar, until she clapped her hands to her head to hold her hair on. Her ears buzzed until she wanted to reach inside them and somehow scratch the itch of it off.

When it died down, there was dead silence. She gripped the edge of the stone wall by the door, her body tingling everywhere. Her nipples felt tight against her bra. Her skin hungered to be rubbed very hard.

Gabriel Delange turned like a lion who had just finished chastising his cubs and spotted her.

Her heart thumped as if she had been caught out on the savannah without a rifle. Her *fight* instinct urged her to stalk across the small space between them, sink her hands into that thick hair, jerk her body up him, and kiss that mouth of his until he stopped roaring with it.

That would teach him.

And her *flight* option wanted to stretch her arm a little higher on that door, exposing her vulnerable body to be savaged.

She gripped that stone so hard it scraped her palm, fighting both urges.

Gabriel stood still, gazing at her. Behind him, the frozen tableau melted: *petits commis,* waiters, sous-chefs, all returning to their tasks with high-speed efficiency, the dispute evaporated. Someone started cleaning up the fallen dishes. Someone else whipped a prepped plate off the wall, where little prongs allowed them to be stacked without touching each other, and began to form another magical creation on top of it.

Jo tried to remember the professional motivation of her visit. She was wearing her let's-talk-about-this-professionally pants. She was wearing her but-this-is-a-friendly-visit little sandals. Given the way her nipples were tingling, she would have preferred that her casually formal blouse have survived her one attempt to eat chocolate in the car while she was wandering around lost for hours, but no . . . her silky pale camisole was all she had left.

Gabriel's eyebrows rose just a little as his gaze flicked over her. Curious. Perhaps intrigued. Cautiously so.

"You're late," he said flatly.

"I had a lot of car trouble," she apologized. It sounded better than saying she had spent hours circling Sainte-Mère and Sainte-Mère-Centre and Sainte-Mère-Vieux-Village, utterly lost. Wait, how did he know she was late? This was a surprise visit. "I'm sorry. I know this is a bad time."

"*Bon, allez.*" He thrust a folded bundle of white cloth at her. She recognized the sturdy texture of it instantly: a chef's jacket. A heavy professional apron followed. His gaze flicked over her again. "Where are your shoes?"

"I—"

"If you drop hot caramel on those painted toenails, I don't want to hear about it. Coming to work without your shoes. I thought Aurélie told me you had interned with Daniel Laurier."   "Uh—"

Eyes blue as the azure coast tightened at the corners. "You made it up to get a chance. *Parfait. And* you're late. That's all I need. Get dressed and go help Thomas with the grapefruit."

Probably she should have told him right then.

But . . . she had been having a hellish two months,

and . . . a sneak peek into Gabriel Delange's kitchens. . . .

A chance to work there through a lunch hour, to pretend she was part of it all. *Not* in an office. Not observing a chef's careful, dumbed-down demonstration. *Part* of it.

She had spent the past two months dealing with hospitals and fear and grief, and he had just handed her happiness on a plate. What was an impassioned food writer to do?

Not the ethical thing, that was for darn sure.

* * *

Available now!

ACKNOWLEDGEMENTS

This novella owes its existence to an invitation from authors Elyssa Patrick and Tamara Morgan to participate in an anthology which they are bringing out for Christmas 2013, a collection of six novellas by different authors around the theme of the title: *Snowbound for Christmas.* I had so many deadline pressures at the time of the invitation that I turned it down, with regret. But, of course, once my creativity felt liberated from the stress of another commitment, I couldn't stop playing with the idea, and within a couple of days, I was carrying this story in my head and had to write it down.

If you want to see what the other authors did with this theme, check out their anthology *Snowbound for Christmas.* With again my enormous thanks to these authors (Gwen Hayes, Louise Hunter, Tamara Morgan, Elyssa Patrick, Maggie Robinson, Marquita Valentine) for their original invitation to be part of it and for all the support.

OTHER BOOKS BY LAURA FLORAND

Amour et Chocolat Series

All's Fair in Love and Chocolate, a novella in *Kiss the Bride*

The Chocolate Thief

The Chocolate Kiss

The Chocolate Rose (also part of La Vie en Roses series)

The Chocolate Touch

The Chocolate Heart

La Vie en Roses Series

Turning Up the Heat (a novella)

The Chocolate Rose (also part of the Amour et Chocolat series)

A Rose in Winter, a novella in *No Place Like Home*

Memoir

Blame It on Paris

ABOUT LAURA FLORAND

Laura Florand was born in Georgia, but the travel bug bit her early. After a Fulbright year in Tahiti, a semester in Spain, and backpacking everywhere from New Zealand to Greece, she ended up living in Paris, where she met and married her own handsome Frenchman. She is now a lecturer at Duke University and very dedicated to her research into French chocolate. For some behind the scenes glimpses of that research, please visit her website and blog at www.lauraflorand.com. You can also join the conversation on Facebook at http://www.facebook.com/LauraFlorandAuthor or email Laura at laura@lauraflorand.com.